THE B

OF BAKED I

CW00828805

Other books by Nick Warburton

THE
BATTLE
OF
BAKED BEAN
ALLEY

NICK WARBURTON

WALKER BOOKS
LONDON

For Jennifer

First published 1992 by Walker Books Ltd
87 Vauxhall Walk, London SE11 5HJ

© 1992 Nick Warburton
Cover illustration © 1992 John Watson

Printed and bound in Great Britain by
Richard Clay Ltd, Bungay, Suffolk

British Library Cataloguing in Publication Data
A catalogue record for this book
is available from the British Library.

ISBN 0-7445-2135-1

CONTENTS

1

I WOKE UP ONE MORNING

I am incensed. Every time I stop and think about it I find myself shaking. Even now my fingers tremble as I hold the pen. I have to do five minutes running on the spot just to stop the steam from shooting out of my ears. Then Mum comes up and smacks the bedroom door with the flat of her hand and steam *is* coming out of her ears. So I have to grovel for a couple of minutes and talk her round. But all the time there's rage rumbling around inside like a storm that's got to break.

"What the flying cracker's going on up here?" Mum says, trying to peer through the gap in the door. Her face moves from side to side as she tries out each eye in turn.

"Nothing," I say. "Why?" And my eyes are all innocent, though my teeth are grinding together in sheer frustration.

"Thump-thump-thump on the ceiling. The neighbours'll be round in a minute. What are you doing?"

"Homework," I say after a moment's hesitation.

"And what kind of homework requires that level of noise, may I ask?"

"P.E. homework. Sorry, Mum. It's over now."

And she goes back downstairs to "East-Enders", placated. But I am not placated. I feel just as bad. I could've told her what's getting under my skin, I suppose, but I cannot trust myself to speak about it without suddenly yelling out a stream of foul abuse that would shock her. And me too, probably.

I try some deep breathing instead. Stay cool, Ivor. Take a grip on yourself. You can beat this. Just be calm, be quiet, breathe deeply and let the mind settle.

You ain't no fool
So be cool, be cool.
In, two three.
Out, with a four and a five
And a long, long six.
Remember the rule
And be cool, be cool.
In, two three.
Out, with a four and a five
And a long, long six.

Several minutes of this and I feel I can at last write down what it is that has caused all this aggravation.

I went down to Oak Green after school, as usual, and it was empty. That's it. That's the cause of all this anger. Simple enough.

I ran over the bridge, rounded the conveniences and there it was. Empty. Not a soul to be seen. Which was more than a bit odd because there's always someone down there playing cricket or flying a kite or something. But not today. Not a soul.

So, Oak Green was empty? Is this enough to send a person into violent running on the spot? No. There's more.

The Green had been fenced off. The giant oak which gives it its name, which spreads its branches out to shade one corner of it, was now on the far side of a line of plastic orange netting. It was like someone roping off part of your own garden. I mean, they can't do things like that. I climb that tree. Dads bowl underarm to little kids on that Green, especially on summer days like this. Tree and Green belong to the people. Even in the Middle Ages, when you'd get your limbs ripped off for pinching half a bread roll or something, they used to let you graze your pigs on the common land. Even black-hearted Norman barons let you do that. They certainly didn't pen your pigs behind a dirty great line of orange plastic fencing.

Anyway, I stood there for a while with my mouth open. Then I saw a man in a grey suit scuttling along the inside of the fence. He wore a plastic helmet and was dragging a wind-up tape-measure behind him. He had a grey, ratty face with an unpleasant sneer on it. Honestly. I'm not just saying that because of what he turned out to be. That is really how he looked. After every few darts along the fencing he stopped to note things down in a little book. I waited till he drew level with me. Be shrewd, I thought. If I start asking about the Green straight off he might tell me to shove off. Start with something casual and harmless.

"Excuse me," I said.

"Shove off."

"I only wanted to ask what the plastic helmet's for?"

"What are they usually for?" asked rat man.

"To protect your head when things fall on it."

"Right. And that's what this one's for."

"But there's nothing here to fall on your head," I said.

He peered at me suspiciously. I glanced at his notebook and saw his name printed on the cover: J. Britch.

"There will be soon," he said. "When the building starts. So push off while it's still safe."

"Push off?"

"Yes. Push off."

"But what are you doing?"

"What's it look like, sonny? I'm measuring up."

"What for?"

"To find out how big it is."

"The Green? But ... why?"

"You're full of questions, aren't you? I'm measuring it up so that Turnovers know exactly how big they can make it."

"Make what?"

"What do you think? Baked Bean Alley."

"Baked Bean Alley?"

"Baked Bean Alley. Which is what Turnovers is building here. An extension to the main shop, especially for Turnovers Baked Beans."

"An extension? Just for beans?"

"Regular Baked Beans, Baked Beans with Saucy Sausage, Trim-Waist Beans, Curried Beans with Bacon Bits, Spaghetti Nooses, Tasty Turnovers Tinned Trim-Waist Titbits..."

"You mean, our Green is going to become part of a shop?"

"Yes. Except it's not."

"Not?"

"Not your Green."

"I've played cricket on it. I've climbed that tree."

"Only out of the kindness of Turnovers' heart. This Green belongs to them and it always has. So, now you know, you can do what I suggested in the first place, can't you?"

"What's that?"

"Push off."

And he went back to his measuring, scrabbling round the fencing like a rat. I assure you, like a rat.

They can't do this, I thought. They can't turn my Green into Baked Bean Alley. It's all wrong. People won't stand for it.

"People won't stand for it, you know," I called after him.

"Oh yes they will," he shouted back. "Turnovers have carried out a survey. Public opinion says it doesn't want a Green, it wants Baked Bean Alley. So shove off before I turn nasty."

Before he *turned* nasty? I didn't wait to find out what that would be like. I shoved off and came back to my room.

So here I am, wondering what to do about it and ordering my thoughts into words. And I feel powerless.

2

LOST GREEN BLUES

I sat on my bedroom floor, strumming my
guitar and letting the words pour out. It's what
oppressed people have always done. Turned
their oppression into song. A few chords and
a few heartfelt phrases. Putting all my soul into
the singing. The song began very powerfully:

Well, I went down the Green
And what did I see, waitin' for to meet
  my eyes?
A dirty great fence was what I done
  se-een,
A-blockin' me off from my prize.
Oh yeah.
Well, a rat with a tape
Was a-measurin' land, a-tellin' me to go
  awa-ay.
Well, there ain't never no escape

13

From that kinda thi-ung till we come to
  the Judgement Da-ay!
Oh yeah!
Oh yeah, Turnovers!
Oh yeah, TurnOVERS!
Oh yeah…

And the feeling was definitely there in the song when Mum came banging on the door again.

"Ivor? Have you got that cat in there?"

"Cat? What cat?"

"Next door's cat. Let him go. It's cruel to keep him against his will."

"I haven't got any cat…"

"Then what's all the racket?"

"It's not a racket," I explained. "It's a protest song."

"You haven't got anything to protest about, Ivor. I'm the one who should be protesting. Me and the neighbours. About that horrible noise."

Her head came round the door and she gave the guitar an unfriendly look.

"Don't tell me," she said. "Music home-work."

"That's right, Mum. I have to do a protest song for music."

"Then why don't you write it down? It'll do a lot more good and it won't interfere with 'One Man and his Dog'."

"Who?"

14

"On telly, Ivor. As you well know."

"Sorry, Mum. Finished now."

And back downstairs she went. But I wasn't too put out this time because I could see at once that she'd got a point. Not about the neighbours or "One Man and his Dog", but about writing it down. That's exactly what I should've been doing. A written protest to send, not to some rat with a tape-measure and a notebook, but directly to the Top Man at Turnovers.

A letter to Turnovers...

Dear Mr Turnover,
What the devil do you think...

No. No, I felt that was a little too sharp. It was what I wanted to say, of course, but it was likely to put the man off. I wanted him to read the letter, not chuck it aside after the first line.

Dear Mr Turnover,
Although I am still at school...

No, that was worse. He wouldn't take any notice of someone still at school. He'd bin that even before he knew it was a protest. I had to be more subtle. Use clever arguments and well-chosen words so he'd find himself interested by the letter and unable to stop reading.

15

Dear Mr Turnover,

I wonder what makes you so sure that this town needs a Baked Bean Alley? I myself have never noticed a shortage of baked beans. They're always there when I want them – which, by the way, I find isn't very often – and I certainly wouldn't attend a Baked Bean Alley specially to get them. In particular I would shun such a place if it was built on the green land which ordinary people have used for their recreation for as long as anyone can remember.

Down the ages, people have flown their kites and played cricket on that Green, and climbed its magnificent oak in a happy healthy fashion, ignorant of the fact that the vast shadow of some shopping baron – you, Mr Turnover – was about to descend and snatch away their rights.

I mentioned these points to Mr J. Britch, the man you sent on to the Green to measure up, and all I got from him was abuse and lame excuses. He told me that Turnovers had public opinion on their side. I very much doubt it. All right-thinking people will prefer a Green on which they can romp, to a mountain of tins full of dangerous additives. You can't pull the wool over my eyes, young though I may be, Mr Turnover.

It's this sort of bullying act that stirs up the ordinary people of this country to protest.

Lost Green Blues

Feelings are running pretty high, as you will see from the enclosed song, "Lost Green Blues", written by someone who does not intend to stand aside and watch the bulldozers plough up this common land. I shall be very interested to know what you intend to do about these objections.

Yours etc.

This was not bad. Not bad at all. Which was not surprising, because it took me three evenings to write. (Mum came up to my room several times to find out why things were so quiet.) It put my case perfectly clearly – the rights of the people against a mountain of baked beans – and it asked some pretty nifty questions. Also, of course, it was backed up by the song, "Lost Green Blues", which was bound to make the man think.

3

LETTERS OF PROTEST

A letter from Turnovers arrived. About time too, I thought. They'd had mine for over a week. I took it up to my room to read. This could be an important document, I thought, maybe even a *historical* document. Certainly it was too important to take in while Mum was going on about what I wanted for breakfast and would I take that disgusting shirt off so it could be washed.

It was a very classy envelope, I must say. Turnovers splashed in red across the top, and my name and address in thick black typing. Yes, this was very promising. Not some dashed-off note just to keep me quiet. It was obvious they'd taken it all very seriously. And it read "Mr I. Demetrius". *Mr.* They probably thought my letter was from some key person in the community. A solicitor or a doctor or something. Which proved it was worth going to all that trouble. The respectful look of this envelope was a very good sign. I held it between my fingers and wondered what the letter inside would say. I felt I'd achieved something here and I didn't want to rush the moment of triumph.

I opened the envelope and took out the letter.

It was neatly folded twice and on stiff, creamy paper. But much shorter than I expected. I could see at a glance that there were only a couple of lines. Perhaps Mr Turnover simply wanted to arrange a meeting to talk things over.

Dear Mr Demetrius,
There is no Mr Turnover and it is a waste of time writing to him. Even if he did exist he would've found your letter a boring joke.
Yours sincerely,
R. Trussett (Security)

A boring joke? This couldn't be right. But wait. A P.S.

P.S. You're wrong about the additives. We at Turnovers go out of our way to make our beans healthy and natural.

Rubbish! Healthy beans? *Rubbish!*

They didn't even return my song. Turnovers, though they may not have known it, had declared war on me. And my blood was up.

So, there's no Mr Turnover, I thought. Well, that's not going to stop me. There must be someone in charge. All I have to do is find out who it is and write a personal letter to him. So, after school, disguised as an innocent shopper, I headed straight for the enemy camp and made a few investigations.

This wasn't as easy as I thought. Turnovers is a mega-market. Each section is twice the size of any other shop I've ever seen and the whole place is probably bigger than some small countries. I decided that the best way to find the man at the top would be to choose the biggest section, see the boss of that and ask him who his boss was.

The biggest section is probably Trends of the Earth, Turnovers' own garden centre, which is about as large as Lord's Cricket Ground but built entirely of plastic and shiny steel. There was a young man in a Turnovers overall hanging around at the entrance so I sauntered up to him and asked a casual question, like any ordinary passer-by.

"Excuse me, but are you in charge?"

"Yes."

I was a bit suspicious of this. He looked too young to be in charge of a place like Trends of the Earth. You probably have to work your way up the Turnovers ladder for forty years to be in charge of something like that. You probably have to be grey or bald and wear a suit and smoke cigars.

"Trolleys," he said suddenly.

"Pardon?"

"What I'm in charge of. Parking trolleys."

"Ah. And is someone in charge of you?"

"Yes. Mr Lithgoe. He's the Trolley Superintendent."

"And his boss is…?"

"Mrs Pargetter. Head of Trends of the Earth (Entrance)."

"I see."

It's going to take hours at this rate, I thought, and I wasn't far wrong. But the young man in charge of trolley-parking knew all the answers. He told me that Mrs Pargetter worked for Mr Lumley, Managing Director of Floor Space (Trends of the Earth), who was under Mr Moat, Superintendent of Garden Furniture (Trends of the Earth), who answered to…

"What I really want to know," I said, interrupting him, "is who is in charge of the whole lot?"

"What, the whole of Trends of the Earth?"

"Yes."

He sucked in his breath. "Ah," he said. "Hmm. That's a bit tricky, that one is. I did know once but, as we never see him, it's sort of slipped my mind. Mrs Pargetter might know…"

"Ah."

"But she's on holiday."

"Oh."

"Why do you want to know?"

"Well, I just thought the Head of Trends of the Earth might be able to tell me who runs the whole place."

"The whole place?"

"Yes. Turnovers."

"The whole of Turnovers? I doubt it. Oh no, I shouldn't think so. There aren't many people important enough to know someone like that."

"So you can't help me, then?"

"No," he said. "It doesn't look as if I can. Sorry."

So there I was with a protest to make and nobody to send it to. I was sure they wouldn't take any notice unless I put *somebody*'s name on the envelope. What could I do? How could I make my protest felt if I couldn't even make it heard?

I was trailing off home and feeling pretty fed up when the young man in charge of trolley-parking called out after me.

"You could always ask the owner, I suppose."

"Who?"

"The owner of Turnovers. The owner might

22

know who's in charge of the whole thing."

"Yes, but how am I going to find out who the owner is?"

"Who the owner is?" he laughed. "Well, everyone knows who the owner of Turnovers is!"

"Do they?"

"Of course they do. It's Lady Blitherwicke of Blitherwicke Hall."

4

ENLISTING THE TROOPS

At last I felt I'd made some proper progress in my fight to save Oak Green, found something I could really get my teeth into. Lady Blitherwicke.

It didn't surprise me that Turnovers was owned by an aristocrat. I mean, it was just like the Middle Ages all over again. Norman barons doing nasty things to the English peasants. (Except, as I said before, even Norman barons drew the line at fencing off common land.) Very likely Lady Blitherwicke had a pint or two of Norman blood in her somewhere. After all, Blitherwicke had a French sort of ring to it, I thought.

Anyway, dealing with a modern baron (or baroness) was going to be a lot easier than dealing with all those Heads of This and Heads of That at Turnovers. All I had to do was persuade Lady Blitherwicke to leave our Green alone and the Green *would* be left alone. Well and truly. A snap of the aristocratic fingers and the plastic orange fencing would be wound up, the chain-saws would remain silent, and ratty little J. Britch with his tape-measure would, himself, have to push off.

This time, though, I was determined not to make the mistake of putting the whole story in my letter. It would be better just to write and ask if I could *see* Lady Blitherwicke. Then maybe I'd take my guitar along and actually sing "Lost Green Blues" to her.

Except that, as an aristocrat, she probably didn't like that kind of bluesy soul music. I wondered what she did like. Hunting horns, probably. No doubt she galloped all over the place on a massive horse, murdering foxes and whipping peasants to left and right with her riding crop. Probably built like an upright bulldog with a diamond-studded collar and a voice that could break plates.

I began to wonder whether I should write the whole story after all. See what sort of a reaction I'd get first. After all, I didn't want to get horse-whipped *and* lose the Green. That wouldn't have done anyone any good.

But no. These were the thoughts of a craven coward. I was going to face this battle-axe in her own den and I would refuse to be afraid of her.

I spent some time composing a battle hymn
to steady my nerves.

Well, I ain't afraid
Of no fox-huntin' dame,
And I ain't a-scared of her frown.
She's a six-foot woman
With a load of dough
But she ain't a-gonna get me down.
Oh Lady Blitherwicke
Of Blitherwicke Hall,
You can get your whip and your gun
But little ol' me's
Gonna mosey along
And make a mess of your fun.

There was more but I heard a thumping on
the wall – from next door, not downstairs –
so I stopped. I couldn't risk being grounded
when I had a battle to organize.

It made sense to find out all I could about
this Blitherwicke woman. Forewarned is fore-
armed, as they say. The best person to ask
about this was Mum. She had scrapbooks full
of stuff about aristocrats and royals. We had
enough Fergie and Lady Di mugs on the shelves
downstairs to supply a large restaurant.

Mum was very keen to fill me in on all the
details about Lady Blitherwicke and I made
the following few notes:

The Lady Blitherwicke File
*Five or six kilometres out of town stands
the estate of Lady Blitherwicke, owner of
Turnovers. It is surrounded by Lady Blitherwicke's fields and hedgerows. One of Lady
Blitherwicke's rivers runs through the middle
of it. Lady Blitherwicke's deer roam in and out
of it and the birds which fly over it are probably Lady Blitherwicke's because they never
perch on a single twig or patch of grass that
does not belong to her.*

*Owning all this is not an easy thing. It tires
Lady Blitherwicke out and she seems to spend
most of her time indoors with her feet up.*

(Mum hadn't actually seen her and nor had
anyone else Mum knew. Which fitted in with
the rest of the Turnovers bosses.)

And that was about it. Nothing about fox-
hunting or riding crops. What this woman was
actually like remained a mystery, so there was
nothing for it but to write my letter and see
what happened.

In the mean time, I mentioned my Campaign
to Save the Green to Rob at school. Rob would
have been a very good person to have on my
side. He's the sort who gets things done. He
seems a bit laid back about life but he's actually very organized and efficient and has a very
good dress sense. He wears all the stuff we

have to wear for school but still manages to look cool. I can't work out how he does it. He even makes the school badge look like a designer label. And people listen to him the way they don't listen to me. If Rob said we had to do something about Turnovers taking Oak Green, people would sit up and take notice. Rob doesn't do much himself but he does get other people doing things for him. So I thought it would be pretty shrewd to get him interested in the Turnovers caper.

He was flicking though his *Financial Times* when I found him.

"Have you heard?" I asked. "What they're doing on the Green?"

"Sure."

"Turning it into a Baked Bean Alley."

"Sure."

"I mean, ordinary people use that Green."

"Sure."

"And once it's stacked full of baked beans, well, I mean, they won't be able to, will they?"

"No," he said. "Shame."

"We ought to do something about it. Protest. Get organized."

He looked up from his paper as if he were hearing me for the first time.

"Sorry, pal," he said. "Not me."

"No?"

"No. The old man's got shares in Turnovers. In my name."

"Yes, but…"

"So I don't want to stir things up, do I?"

"Don't you?"

"Sure I don't. That would be standing in the way of progress. We don't want to do that, do we?"

"Don't we?"

"I don't."

"No. Right. Well, be seeing you, Rob."

"Sure."

And he went back to reading his paper. Leaving me feeling a bit flat, a bit on a limb. I was even thinking that maybe it was a waste of time protesting at all. Maybe I was wrong to stand in the way of progress. That's the kind of effect Rob has on you. Well, on me, anyway.

I was wandering along the corridor, deep in these thoughts, when I came across this small figure like a lost armadillo. Jessica. Of course, I thought. *Jessica.*

Jessica isn't really like an armadillo. It's just her jacket that looks like one. She wears all these protest badges. All over the front and the back, all down the sleeves. So many badges that she can hardly bend her arms. Nuclear waste, rain forests, whales, smoking, motorways. You name it. She's not such an organized person as Rob, but she does care about things. And get things done, in her own way.

"Oh, Ivor," she said when she saw me. "I'm not sure I know what it's about any more."

"Life?" I said. Jessica is always worrying about what life means, and what she should do about it.

"No," she said. "The timetable. I can't remember where I'm supposed to be."

"You're supposed to be in History. We both are."

"Oh, thank you," she said, chewing her lip. "Upstairs History or downstairs History?"

"Upstairs. Follow me."

She swung her bag on her shoulder and followed, the badges rattling together as she moved.

"I was thinking of starting a protest movement myself, Jessica," I said casually.

"Really? I didn't know you cared about things."

"Of course I care about things."

"Well, you didn't sign my petition about badgers crossing the motorway."

"Oh. Didn't I?"

"Everyone else in the form did. What's your protest about?"

"Turnovers."

"Oh, yes. I've protested about them."

"Have you? That's good because..."

"I wrote to them about recycling tins. It's something they ought to be doing, you know. It's their responsibility just as much as it is ours."

"Oh yes. I agree. It's just that I could do with

some support over..."

"It worked, too," said Jessica. "They're building a new Baked Bean Alley and it's going to have a recycling plant in it. Isn't that marvellous?"

"Yes. Marvellous."

So that was that. As far as the Campaign to Save the Green was concerned, I was on my own. So be it, then, I thought. A one-man campaign for the rights of the people. And the people could thank me for it when I'd won. If they could be bothered.

5

STIRRING THE SILVER SPOON

A letter arrived from Blitherwicke Hall. It was brought to the door by a plump, red-faced, maid on a bike. Apparently Lady Blitherwicke didn't believe in trusting things to the post. The maid was fairly puffed after her ride and wasn't able to say anything, so she handed the letter over without a word, climbed back on her bike and wobbled off. Not very impressive, I thought, but Mum was so excited at the idea of someone who worked for a real-live Lady coming to our door that she had to stretch out on the sofa with a wet flannel over her eyes with the sound on the telly turned down.

"Whatever are you up to, Ivor?" she asked me, clutching her head. "Getting letters from Lady Blitherwicke?"

"Oh, you know," I said. "I sort of ... wrote to her and she ... just sort of wrote back."

"But why? I mean, what about?"

"About the Green, actually."

"The Green? What's the Green got to do with it?"

"Turnovers are turning it into a Baked Bean Alley..."

"Really? That sounds nice."

"And I've written to Lady Blitherwicke to see if she'll stop it."

"What!" Mum jackknifed off the sofa and flung the flannel from her face in one move. It flew across the room, smacked the window and stuck there for a second. "You did what?"

"Well, I just sort of..."

Suddenly she was full of energy, pacing up and down, her eyes flashing and her arms waving about. And, strangely, the headache had gone.

"Whatever possessed you to do such a thing! Insulting the landed gentry like that. You are to write and say sorry, Ivor, do you hear me? What must the poor lady think?"

"I've only asked to see her," I said. "She doesn't know what I want."

"Thank goodness for that."

"And, anyway, I think it's terrible to build a Baked Bean Alley on our Green."

"Listen to me, my boy, if Lady Blitherwicke wants to build a Baked Bean Alley on the Green, then she's perfectly entitled to do so. If she wanted to turn it into a giant toadstool and perch a thousand garden gnomes on it, she could do just that. What you don't seem to realize is that Lady Blitherwicke is a Lady. A *real* Lady. And real Ladies do what Ladies want to do."

Mum can go on like this for hours once she's got the steam up. You don't have to say anything. Just stand there looking at the carpet and listening. I fiddled with the envelope while I waited for her to wind down.

"You're not going up there, Ivor. You're not going to insult Lady Blitherwicke in her own mansion. I'd never live with the shame. In fact, you're not going up there at all. I forbid it. I can't run the risk. You'd call things by their common names and very probably ask to use the bog and I don't know what. No son of mine is going to put me through an ordeal like that. Poor Lady Blitherwicke."

By this time my finger had fiddled open the envelope and somehow pulled out Lady Blitherwicke's letter. I glanced down to see what it said. It was written in scratchy blue ink and was rather hard to read.

Dear Mr Demetrius …

"Ivor, you're not listening to me. You'll never learn anything if you don't listen. What have I told you about respect for the Upper Classes?"

Stirring the Silver Spoon

... my man Stote will take care of ...

"They've got blue blood. They're born with it and it means they know the right way to behave. Perfect manners. Perfect taste. And, anyway, she'd never agree to see a peasant like you..."

... next Wednesday at four-thirty ...

"You do the rude thing by instinct, even though I've tried to drum it out of you. If you'd been born with a drop of blue blood... What are you staring at?"

She snatched the letter out of my hand and read it, moving her head fiercely from side to side to follow Lady Blitherwicke's scrawl.

"Argh!" she screeched. "Argh! She's asked you to tea!"

She collapsed backwards on to the sofa and the letter fluttered to the carpet. I picked it up.

Dear Mr Demetrius, it said, *Thank you for your letter. Are you by any chance one of the Northamptonshire Demetriuses? I think you must be. Do come to tea. My man Stote will take care of all the arrangements but next Wednesday at four-thirty would be a good time. Yours, Marigold Blitherwicke.*

The room had gone quiet. Mum was clutching her head again. She began to moan softly.

"You'll have to have your hair cut," she said as if to herself. "And wear a white shirt with a tie. Good grief. You haven't got a tie! Run next door and borrow one from Mr Gooch and tell him not the one he keeps his gardening trousers up with. Tell him it's got to be smart because you're going to tea with Lady Blither-wicke."

6

LADY BLITHERWICKE

When Wednesday came, I left Mum on the sofa with a couple of asprins.

"Make sure you go to the toilet first, Ivor," she muttered. "If you have to use her Ladyship's facilities I'll die of shame and you needn't bother to come back. You can run away to sea or something."

So, of course, as soon as I set foot on the very first step of Blitherwicke Hall, I had this great desire to go to the loo. I wouldn't have done if Mum hadn't made so much fuss about it. I know I wouldn't.

Stote, the butler, let me in, peering down at me with his thin, yellow face as he held open the great door. He lifted one eyebrow in surprise when he saw how young I was but he didn't say anything. He didn't have to: you could see it in his face. A *child*? Here? How disgusting.

Nevertheless, I thought it would be better to ask Stote about the loo, rather than Lady Blitherwicke herself. Only I couldn't think of the right word. Not loo, certainly, and probably not toilet or gents. Maybe lavatory, but that sounded daft to me: I couldn't bring myself to say it. The only thing I could think of was what Mum had said about "facilities". I practised the word a few times in my head, but by the time I felt I could actually say it out loud without sounding too much of a nelly, we had climbed a broad staircase and Stote was tapping at a pair of ornate double doors. And a thin voice on the other side was bidding us enter.

Lady Blitherwicke came as a bit of a surprise. She wasn't large and strapping. Nor did she smack her jodhpurs with a riding crop all the time. In fact, she wasn't wearing jodhpurs at all. She had on a pale blue, fluffy cardigan and a flowery dress. And she was small with a nest of white hair which had pins sticking out of it. And the room surprised me, too. I hadn't expected it to be so ... well, shabby.

She stood at a large bay window with her back to us, peering through a telescope at her rolling fields and distant woods.

"Ivor Demetrius," announced Stote in a cracked voice before silently backing out.

I waited. Lady Blitherwicke didn't turn round or move a muscle. The need for the facilities was becoming desperate. I cleared my throat and was about to ask when she spoke.

"Has he gorn?"

I wasn't sure what to say.

"Stote. Has he gorn?"

"Yes, your Ladyship ... er, ma'am."

"Good-o," she said, spinning round. "He really does give one the willies, that man. Can't do a thing when he's around. He's always tickin' one orf, don't you know. Makes one so nervous."

She gave me a little smile and held out her hand.

"Marigold Blitherwicke," she said. "Pleased to meet you. You're one of the Northamptonshire Demetriuses, I believe."

"No," I said. "I'm one of the ordinary Demetriuses, from town. Just up the road. I don't know anyone from Northampton."

I tried to clamp my knees together and wriggle towards her to shake hands.

"I say, are you all right?"

"Yes. Oh yes. Fine, thank you. I just wanted to have a word about..."

"Do you need a pee or somethin'?" Lady Blitherwicke asked with a frown. "You look as though you do."

"Well, yes, as a matter of fact. Yes, I do. Sorry."

"Right. Through that door, down the corridor, second on your left. Give the door a good heave – it's solid oak – and you'll find the what's-name up a couple of steps. I'll wait here for you. Orf you go."

When I got back she was peering through her telescope again. I thought she'd heard me come back into the room but obviously she hadn't because, when I gave a little cough, she jumped violently and sent the telescope spinning on its tripod.

"What?" she said. "Oh, it's you. Thought it was Stote come back. He does sometimes, you know. Creeps along to see what I'm up to. Take a seat."

We sat down together and she started to chat to me. It was all very easy, as if I were always popping in and she knew me quite well. In fact, things seemed so easy that I thought I'd come straight out with my protest about the Green.

"Could I have a word about Turnovers, Lady Blitherwicke?"

She looked at me and blinked. As if I'd suddenly started speaking in a foreign language. Then, instead of answering my question, she asked one of her own.

"Do you know what I was up to just now?"

"No, Lady Blitherwicke."

"Lookin' through my telescope. And do you know, everythin' I can see through that blasted thing belongs to me. Amazin', isn't it? Trees, fields, the blessed lot."

"You must be very well off," I said. "I was just wondering about…"

"What? Well orf? It's a bally nuisance most of the time, let me tell you. Ownin' things. A bally nuisance. Do you own many things, young Demetrius?"

"Not many, no, Lady Blitherwicke."

"You ought to keep it like that. Lot of jolly nonsense. People rollin' up to the door to tell me about things I own. Fill in this form, fill in that, sign here, there and everywhere. Can't stand it. D'you know what I was lookin' for through my telescope just now, young Demetrius?"

"No."

She leaned towards me and lowered her voice.

"I was looking for Jerkin."

"Jerkin?"

"Mrs Jerkin. My maid. Sent her orf on her bike this mornin'. Stote doesn't know, of course. Don't tell Stote, nosy old duffer."

"No, of course not."

"Sent her orf to the library, you see. I send her orf every week. To the library."

"What for?" I asked.

"To borrow books, of course. Library books. I love my library books and I take great care of them. Particularly because they *don't* belong to me. They're the only things in the area that I don't own, you see. So I borrow them. Lovely little beggars, library books. D'you ever borrow them?"

She laughed suddenly and, just as suddenly, stopped and looked round, as if someone might be spying on her.

"I say," she said. "D'you want a biscuit?"

"Erm ... well." I wasn't quite sure what to say. In fact, I wasn't quite sure what to think about all this. Every time I tried to mention Turnovers she veered round to a new subject. And I couldn't tell whether she was doing it on purpose or not.

"Go on," she said. "Have a biscuit. One doesn't usually get biscuits on a Wednesday but one might just pull it orf if a guest asked for one."

"All right," I said. "I'd like a biscuit. And then I'd like to talk about..."

"Good-o."

Lady Blitherwicke clapped her hands together and skipped over to a length of tubing in the corner. She snatched it up, blew down it and then held it to her ear. Stote's tiny voice came floating out.

"Yes?"

"Stote? Is that you?"

"Of course it's me."

"My guest would like a biscuit."

The tube fell silent for some moments.

"Did you hear what I said, Stote?"

"He'll have to come down here for it," said Stote.

Lady Blitherwicke pulled a face at me.

"Would you mind?" she said. "Stote says you'll have to fetch it yourself. One can't ask him to bring it up. He's in such a fearfully crabby mood today."

7

STOTE TAKES THE BISCUIT

It took a long time to find the kitchens where Stote had his lair. Down stairs, some broad and some twisting, through doors both great and small, up and down corridors. Once or twice I found myself outside Blitherwicke Hall altogether and had to retrace my steps. Eventually, however, I pushed open a low door that looked as if it belonged to a cupboard and found myself looking down a flight of stone steps into a cold, gloomy kitchen. Stote was sitting at a large table doing a crossword. He looked up at me and wrinkled his nose.

"You're the one who's been demanding biscuits, I suppose," he said.

"Well," I said, "Lady Blitherwicke thought she might…"

"She had a biscuit yesterday. She's not getting one today."

"Oh. I see. Actually, I was trying to ask her about Turnovers..."

"Turnovers?" said Stote, and he leaned back in his chair and spat into a dark corner. "What do you want to know about Turnovers, sonny?"

Just then, Mrs Jerkin burst in at the back door. A cycle clip snapped off her ankle and scuttered over the stone floor.

"What *do* you want cycle clips for, you daft old crow?" snapped Stote. "Cycle clips are for trousers. It's a waste of time to put cycle clips on bare ankles."

Mrs Jerkin was even redder in the face than when she'd delivered Lady Blitherwicke's letter to me before. She leaned against the doorpost heaving for breath. I could just see a couple of books beneath a teacloth in her shopping basket.

"Her Ladyship says you're to get this boy a biscuit," said Stote, eyeing the books suspiciously. "Go on. Get a move on. The boy wants his biscuit."

Mrs Jerkin gave me a wheezy smile. It was quite a relief after Stote's growling and spitting. She dumped her basket on the table and waddled over to one of the huge cupboards.

"Oh dear," she said. "Biscuits, biscuits. I'm sure we had biscuits in here yesterday."

"Of course we did," said Stote. "I put a fresh packet of Bobbly-Oddbods there myself."

"Hmm. Let me see. Bobbly-Oddbods, Bobbly-Oddbods..."

"Exactly," said Stote. "Bobbly-Oddbods – a New Biscuit Experience, crammed with Country Goodness."

"No," said Mrs Jerkin. "No Bobbly-Oddbods in here."

"There must be. You get fifteen Bobbly-Oddbods in a packet. I've had six and you've had two..."

Mrs Jerkin swallowed. "Which means," she said. "Which means..."

"That crafty old bag upstairs has had the rest!" said Stote with a thump of his fist on the kitchen table. A bread knife rattled on a thick chopping-board.

"Mr Stote, you can't call her Ladyship a crafty old bag ..."

"Shut your trap and see if there are any Tum-crumb Creams."

"No," said Mrs Jerkin from inside the cupboard. "I don't think so."

"Oh dear, oh dear," said Stote. "What about Blocka-chockas?"

"No."

"Biffi-Wheatie Bars?"

"Well, there's a Biffi-Wheatie Bar wrapper but no actual Biffi-Wheatie Bar."

Stote banged both fists on the table.

When I got back to Lady Blitherwicke her eyes were twinkling with expectation.

"Did you get them?" she said.

"I'm afraid not. They've run out."

"Oh pish and tush. Run out? Blitherwicke Hall run out of biscuits? This can't be true."

"I'm afraid it is. There doesn't seem to be very much food down there at all."

She sank into her worn armchair in a sulk. She looked so crestfallen that I began to feel sorry for her. Mrs Jerkin had felt sorry for her, too. She'd checked all the cupboards and found nothing but salt and herbs and spices.

"Mrs Jerkin said she could rustle up a little snack with the things she's got," I told her. "A Spicy Herb Rissole. Or a Herby Rissole in a Spicy Sauce. Or Salt 'n' Vinegar Spice Slices. Or Herb Burgers with a Salt 'n' Spice Dip..."

"That's bally good of her, young Demetrius," she said wistfully. "But it's not quite what one had in mind. I don't suppose Stote's plannin' to go shoppin' at all, is he?"

"I'm afraid not. He said he'd rather wait till Saturday, when he usually goes."

(What he'd actually said was, "If the silly old bat thinks I'm going shopping just so she can stuff her daft face with Bobbly-Oddbods, she's got another think coming.")

Then it struck me. This was the perfect chance to introduce the subject of Turnovers... I could take her there, give her a shopper's-eye-view of the place, then take her to see the noble old oak tree she was going to have hacked down to make way for Baked Bean Alley.

"You could go shopping yourself," I said.

"What?"

"You could go to Turnovers yourself if you wanted some more biscuits."

"Go shoppin'? Me? My father was a Knight of the Bathtub. The Blitherwickes don't go shoppin'."

"Not even to Turnovers?"

"Where?"

"Turnovers. The megastore in town."

"Never heard of it."

"But you own it."

"Do I?"

"Yes. It belongs to you," I said. "You must have been there before, Lady Blitherwicke."

"I couldn't go shoppin' in Turnovers, Demetrius. Stote would never stand for it."

"Then don't tell him."

"What?" she said, springing to her feet.

"Don't tell him. Go in secret."

"Me? In Turnovers? What would people say?"

"They needn't know. You could go in disguise."

"I say!"

She flopped back into her armchair and her brow creased. For a moment I thought I'd said too much. I could just imagine myself being thrown out of Blitherwicke Hall by the scruff of my neck. Stote would've enjoyed that.

"I say," she said again. "What a spiffin' idea. Me, shoppin'. In disguise. Absolutely top-hole. Let's do it!"

8

TURNOVERS: GETTING IN

Before we could set off on the shopping expedition, Lady Blitherwicke said she needed time to sort out her disguise. She liked the idea of the disguise. In fact, she liked it so much that she stopped worrying about the absence of biscuits altogether.

"Whatever you do," she told me before I left Blitherwicke Hall, "don't let that creep Stote know about our little scheme. He'd never let one go if he heard about it."

I thought that was odd. She was the Lady; she was supposed to run the place. And yet she let the butler order her around. It was as if she were scared of him.

Anyway, I didn't tell Stote and, when I got home, I didn't tell Mum either. She was desperate to know what had happened, whether I'd done anything rude and ill-mannered or mentioned bogs or Baked Bean Alley.

"No, Mum," I said. "I didn't say a word about Baked Bean Alley." Which was the truth.

I'd arranged to meet Lady Blitherwicke outside Turnovers at six the next day. She'd said I'd know her because she'd be wearing a hat with two feathers stuck in it, but you get crowds and crowds of people at Turnovers and at least half of them wear silly hats.

Actually it wasn't that difficult to spot her in the end. She looked just the same as she did when I first met her – sort of dithery with her fluffy cardigan and her white hair stuck with pins. There were only three obvious differences. She had a trilby hat (with two long feathers in it) perched on top of the hair; her flowery dress was tucked into a pair of baggy old trousers; and she was wearing a pair of dark glasses with a built-in plastic nose.

"Right, lad," she said when she saw me. "Let's get crackin'. In we jolly well go."

And she marched confidently in the direction of the nearest door. I tried to stop her – after all, I'd been to Turnovers before and knew what it was like – but she was in a state of high excitement, not really listening to anything I said.

When she reached the door she put her hand out to grasp the handle. And couldn't find it.

"Dashed ridiculous," she said. "How can

one shop if one can't even get in?"

I pointed out that the doors at Turnovers were automatic.

"Ah," said Lady Blitherwicke, moving back so that she could make a good, brisk approach. "Splendid. Dashed clever idea."

"The thing is, though," I said, "this door is..."

"Say no more, young Demetrius. I understand. You don't have to explain Technology to me."

And she made her good, brisk approach. And came to a sudden halt. She slid down the glass door, her false nose squashed into her face, her hat toppling off her head.

"This is the way out, Lady Blitherwicke," I explained as I tried to haul her to her feet. "The door only opens from the other side."

"Then why didn't you tell me, you bally young cad?" she demanded.

She was sitting on the floor, leaning against the door. Which meant that she didn't see the trolley rattling towards her from the other side. In fact, the first thing Lady Blitherwicke knew about that trolley was the swishing open of the door. She rolled backwards into the shop. The second thing she knew was the front wheel running over her hand.

The trolley lurched as it struck her fingers and three or four tins of dog food tumbled about her ears.

"What the dickens are you doing down there, you fool?" barked the fierce-looking woman who was wheeling the trolley.

But Lady Blitherwicke didn't hear. The doors had closed. She was inside the shop and the fierce woman was outside. The woman looked at me and raised her eyebrows.

"As if shopping isn't hard enough these days," she said, "without hooligans like that flinging themselves under your wheels!"

Still, Lady Blitherwicke *was* inside Turnovers which was what she wanted – although she wasn't inside for long. A uniformed man marched up to her and placed a heavy hand on her shoulder. I saw him ask her a brief question. I saw her face go blank. She began delving deep into the pockets of the baggy trousers.

Seconds later she was outside the shop again, helped by a smart shove from the man in the uniform.

"How utterly stupid," she said. "The fool wanted to see my clearance card."

"You need a clearance card to get in," I told her. "They give people one as soon as they go through the door."

"They dashed well didn't give me one," sniffed Lady Blitherwicke.

"That's because you went through the wrong door."

We made our way to the correct door which

swished open as soon as it saw us coming.

"This is more like it," said Lady Blither-wicke. "Now for some proper shoppin'."

Well, not quite, I thought. Now for Security Clearance.

Security Clearance was a small gate guarded by a man with a black peaked cap pulled down over his eyes. He pointed an electronic pointer at Lady Blitherwicke. The electronic pointer turned up some information which set a screen humming and threw green light on the man's face. Or on what we could see of his face. The man made a tutting noise and shook his head.

"Oh dear," he said. "Oh dear, oh dear."

"What is it?" asked Lady Blitherwicke. "What's the matter?"

"Are you Dennis Cantaloup of Ponders End?"

"No," said Lady Blitherwicke. "I'm Lady … I mean I'm er…"

"*Kevin* Cantaloup of *Hermon Hill*," I suggested.

"Really?" said the man, flashing the shiny peak of his cap at Lady Blitherwicke. "And what collar size are you?"

"What collar size?"

"Exactly. And I wouldn't try and pull a fast one, Mr so-called Kevin Cantaloup, because I have an electronic measuring device on my person and can very easily check."

"Sixteen," guessed Lady Blitherwicke.

"Well, what a coincidence! Just the same as Dennis 'no relation' Cantaloup of Ponders End. Also known as Check-out Charlie."

He leaned forward until the peak of his cap was touching the end of Lady Blitherwicke's plastic nose. The name on his cap twinkled in brass letters: Sergeant R. Trussett. I've seen that name somewhere before, I thought. Not in brass letters but in thick, black type on smooth cream notepaper. Of course. This was the very man who'd written that abusive letter to me. I had a good mind to step in and let him know what I thought, big as he was. But I controlled myself.

"And I don't suppose we were planning to smuggle any more shampoo out of Turnovers this evening, were we, sir?" he said.

"Bally sauce," muttered Lady Blitherwicke. "I most certainly wasn't. Were you?"

"Don't try and be witty with me, Den. I'm too fast on my feet."

"No, no," I said. "She ... I mean *he* means he's only come in for some sauce. Turnovers Fruit'n'Spice Squirter Special. Mmm. Everyone's favourite."

Sergeant Trussett straightened his back and thrust his jaw out in an aggressive fashion. But he seemed satisfied.

"All right," he said, handing us two clearance cards. "He can go in, just this once."

"Thank you very much, officer."

"But I'll be watching him. Like a hawk."

Getting a trolley was not much easier than getting clearance cards. The trolleys were all chained together and it wasn't possible to take one unless you dropped a coin in a slot and wrenched a lever. Lady Blitherwicke didn't have much patience. I dropped in a coin and she yanked her trolley free so violently that it almost mowed down a man on a ladder stacking packs of nappies.

Eventually, though, with our clearance cards in our hands, we were able to step into the bright and wonderful world of Turnovers. The happy music and the garish light. The jostling elbows and the nudging trolleys. It had taken us ages to get this far. But we were in. More or less cleared by Security. With a trolley. Now Lady Blitherwicke could enjoy her very first shopping expedition in earnest.

"Right, my lad, let's head for the biscuits," said Lady Blitherwicke, pushing her trolley straight into the flow of trolley traffic.

"I wouldn't," I said.

"Nonsense, young Demetrius."

She caught sight of the biscuit counter almost at once and gave me a knowing look. But the crowd was sweeping her away.

"Excuse me ... sorry," she said as she tried to swing her trolley round. "Look out ... I beg your pardon, madam. Didn't see you bendin' there..."

You should've heard people moan. The air was full of shoppers moaning – and that endless, sickly-sweet music that Turnovers keep playing.

"What's going on?" someone called. "Why the hold-up?"

"Some idiot's trying to go against the traffic."

"What's the silly old twerp doing?"

"Don't turn round here, you old pilchard!"

Lady Blitherwicke spluttered and fumed but she did manage to turn the trolley round. The biscuit counter, however, was fading into the distance and she couldn't do anything about it. She had to go with the flow. Backwards. And going backwards with a trolley meant we had to face the people we'd just held up. Immediately behind us (or in front of us, now that we were facing backwards) was a thick-set man in a vest. A large, pink child was sitting in his trolley, clashing soup tins together.

"Gallopin' garters, Demetrius," said Lady Blitherwicke. "Looks like one can buy children here. Bally strange idea, that."

"Dad," wailed the child, "I don't like that funny man. He's got a fat nose and he's going backwards. Why's he going backwards, Dad?"

The man scowled at us and Lady Blitherwicke smiled and tried to pretend that she *wanted* to be going backwards, that she was enjoying it.

"What's he laughing at?" grizzled the child. "I don't like him, Dad."

"Why shouldn't he go backwards?" came a familiar voice from behind the man in the vest. "People ought to be free to go backwards if they like."

It was Jessica. She peered at us through the crook of the man's arm.

"Look at that poor old man," she said. "He's confused and… Oh. Ivor."

"Hello, Jessica," I said, bending slightly so I could see through the man's arm, too.

"Are you with that poor old gentleman?"

"Yes, I'm helping her – him – with his shopping."

"That's very noble of you, Ivor. I think you…"

Before she could say another word, the man clamped his arm to his side.

"Do you mind?" he said.

At that point, the traffic surged round a corner into a wide stretch and I was able to give the trolley a spin so we were facing the right direction again. Jessica manoeuvred her trolley next to ours and beamed at us.

"I'm so glad you're helping others, Ivor," she said to me out of the corner of her mouth. "It's such a healthy sign."

9

TURNOVERS: GETTING OUT

We did the complete Turnovers circuit twice after that. And a circuit of Turnovers is rather like a circuit of Brands Hatch, only a little bit longer and not quite so safe. It wasn't because we thought it would be fun. We had no choice. Lady Blitherwicke insisted on driving and she kept steering us into dangerous trolley rapids. Jessica came too, keeping a watchful eye on us. We found ourselves shoved and juddered down aisles of cod bites, tinned raspberries, Very Very Low Fat Lime Peel Yak Yogurt and other places we didn't want to go to. Eventually we came to a quiet bay by some towering shelves of socks and pants.

Of course, Lady Blitherwicke didn't want any socks or pants. She wasn't a socks and pants sort of person. On the other hand, ours was the only empty trolley in Turnovers as far as we could tell.

"One ought to put somethin' in the blasted trolley, laddy," she hissed at me. "Just to look as if one knows what one is doin'. Don't want to draw attention to ourselves, do we?"

A bit late for that, I thought. Especially when one is wearing a large plastic nose.

She picked up a pair of socks and at once a piercing whistle sounded by her ear. She leapt into the air and clutched my arm.

"What the blue blazes is that?" she said.

"An alarm," I told her. "We'd better move on."

She put her head down and tried to speed away but it was no good. Sergeant Trussett was already loping in our direction.

"Well, well, well," he said. "If it isn't my old pal, Check-out Charlie."

"Listen, my good man, I am not Check-out Charlie," said Lady Blitherwicke.

"No, Den. Of course you're not. But you have just picked up a pair of tagged socks, unless I'm much mistaken."

"What's wrong with that?" said Jessica. I could see that her eyes were beginning to sparkle. "This is a shop, isn't it? You have to pick things up if you want to buy them."

"He wants to buy the socks?" asked the Sergeant. "So where's his ticket?"

"Ticket?" asked Lady Blitherwicke. "What ticket?"

"Don't tell me you don't know. You don't just *pick up* a pair of socks, mate. If you want socks, you go to the ticket centre located near the sock department, queue for a ticket, obtain the ticket, take it to the sock shelves and select your socks. Then get your ticket punched. No bother and no alarms going off. What could be simpler than that?"

"Yes," I said. "Thank you. Thanks very much. I think we know what to do now. Sorry to be such a bother…"

"No, Ivor," said Jessica. "You shouldn't put up with that. This is harassment of a senior citizen…"

But I put my head down and trundled us smartly round a corner and out of sight. I was looking for an exit but Lady Blitherwicke caught sight of the biscuit counter and snatched the trolley away from me. She jostled for a place in the queue for tickets to buy biscuits and then jostled for a place in the queue for the biscuits themselves. Or, at least, that's what she thought she was doing.

"Lady Blitherwicke, don't you think we ought to…"

"Don't talk me out of it, you young puppy," she said grimly. "There were Cantaloups – I mean Blitherwickes – at Agincourt and Water-loo. I'm bally well not leavin' without a packet of Bobbly-Oddbods."

"Yes, but this isn't the biscuit…"

"Let him buy the biscuits, Ivor," cut in Jessica. "Can't you see what they mean to him?"

When she got to the front of the queue, Lady Blitherwicke found herself lined up at one of the check-outs. Wedged in between the till and a pile of Special Offer Slinky Green Tights. By the time she realized where she was, it was impossible to back out again.

"Next," said the check-out girl.

She frowned at Lady Blitherwicke who was trying to jiggle the trolley into reverse. Behind her was the man in the vest with his large, pink child perched on his trolley like a figure-head.

"It's that nasty, nasty man, Dad," whined the child.

"Come along, six-four-double-seven," said the girl. "Keep moving!"

"I'm not six-four-double-seven," said Lady Blitherwicke. "I'm Marigold Blither…"

"He's Dennis, I mean *Kevin* Cantaloup," I cut in quickly.

"It says six-four-double-seven on his clearance card so that's who he is as far as I'm concerned," said the girl. "Now what have you got?"

She leaned forward and looked into the trolley.

"A pair of socks?" she sneered. "Is that all you want?"

"Of course not," said Lady Blitherwicke.

"What I really want is a packet of Bobbly-Oddbods but I'll settle for the socks instead."

"This is check-out thirty-nine," said the girl, "not Biscuit Boulevard. You'll have to pay up and go through first. If you want Bobbly-Oddbods you'll have to go back in through Security Clearance…"

"No, no," begged Lady Blitherwicke. "Not that. I'll take the socks. That's all one wants really. Thank you very much."

"So what's the biscuit ticket for?"

"Well, one did want biscuits but one's changed one's mind."

"One can't do that. If one took a biscuit ticket, one'll have to buy some biscuits."

"No," said Lady Blitherwicke wildly. "I don't want any biscuits. Please."

"Oi," said the man in the vest. "He can't come through here with a pair of socks and a biscuit ticket. This is a fifty items or more check-out." And the pink child in his trolley agreed with him.

"That's right," said the girl. "You haven't got enough in that trolley."

"Why don't you leave the poor old boy alone?" said Jessica. "Turnovers shouldn't treat their elderly customers like this. It's disgraceful."

"They shouldn't get in the wrong queue, then, should they?" shouted the girl.

"It's not his fault that the biscuit queue

63

looks the same as the check-out queue," she said.

"Will you shift the old plonker out of the way?" said the man in the vest.

"Don't be so cruel. Can't you see he's in a bad way? Look at his nose..."

"Jessica," I said. "Don't make a fuss. We just want to get out."

"No, Ivor. You shouldn't let them treat this poor old man like this. That nose is an indication that something is wrong. It's a beacon to anyone who's done first aid. He's probably suffering from sudden heat-loss or something."

"Please," I said to the girl. "Can't you let us through?"

"Not with what you've got in that trolley," she said.

"Yes, but..."

She heaved a sigh and pressed a button beneath her counter. Somewhere a bell sounded and the light above her till started to flash on and off. Lady Blitherwicke looked round and saw Sergeant Trussett threading his way grimly towards us. She snatched up some boxes of the Special Offer Slinky Green Tights and tipped them into the trolley.

"There," she said. "I'll take these too."

"Three dozen tights and a pair of socks," said the girl. "You're still twelve items short."

"Flibberty-gibbet," said Lady Blitherwicke

and she grabbed another box of tights.

Jessica was wagging a finger at the man in the vest who was telling her to forget about old men's noses, to keep her own out of other people's business and not to hold up queues. His child was moaning and gathering in breath for a piercing scream. Sergeant Trussett reached the end of the queue and stood on tiptoe to find out what the trouble was.

"Oh no," he cried. "Not you again."

"It's OK, Sarge," said the check-out girl. "He's just about to cough up."

"Cough up?" said Lady Blitherwicke. "I most certainly am not. And you can keep your impertinent remarks to yourself, you hussy."

"She means pay, Lady Bli ... I mean Kevin," I said.

"Oh. Pay. Yes, well, I'm afraid I never handle money. Beastly stuff. You'll have to speak to my man Stote about that."

By this time Sergeant Trussett was breathing heavily through his nose and trying to claw his way past Jessica and the man in the vest, so I dug deep into my pocket.

"It's all right," I said. "I'll pay."

Three pence change I got from that little deal. Three pence change and four dozen Special Offer Slinky Green Tights. I didn't know what Mum was going to make of that. Still, it was just about worth it to get out of Turnovers alive. (We left Jessica discussing

65

noses at the check-out, but she was well able to look after herself.)

I could tell that Lady Blitherwicke was pretty shaken up by her first experience of shopping. Still, I suppose if you've never been shopping in your life, you ought to start on something straightforward, like a packet of wine gums from the corner shop. Going to Turnovers is very much plunging in at the deep end.

I made sure we headed back in the direction of Oak Green.

"Blasted awful place, laddy," Lady Blitherwicke said. "Are you really tellin' me I own all that?"

"Yes, Lady Blitherwicke."

"Awful. Absolutely bally awful."

"You own this too, Lady Blitherwicke," I said as we rounded the side of Trends of the Earth and came face to face with the fenced-in oak.

"What? All this dashed orange plastic? Are you sure?"

"Not only the plastic fence, Lady Blitherwicke," I said. "That lovely old oak behind it. And the Green. Where people fly kites and play cricket."

"Cricket, young Demetrius? Did I ever tell you my old pater, Lord Armitage Blitherwicke, had a couple of games for MCC in his youth?"

"And I still climb that tree in mine, Lady

Blitherwicke. But not for much longer," I explained dolefully. "And no more cricket on Oak Green. Turnovers, that is to say *you*, are planning to build on it."

"Good grief! Am I? What am I plannin' to build?"

"Baked Bean Alley, Lady Blitherwicke."

"Baked Bean Alley? What the blazes is that?"

I paused dramatically. A gigantic yellow digger was chugging backwards through a gap in the fence. It sent belches of black smoke into the trees as it manoeuvred into position, ready to start hacking away at the green, green grass of our precious Oak Green.

"It's a shop," I said. "An extension of Turnovers. Complete with trolleys and check-outs and Security Clearance."

"My sainted aunt!" said Lady Blitherwicke with a quaver in her voice. "I won't have that. By heaven, I won't!"

10

REINFORCEMENTS

Lady Blitherwicke stood beside me and saw all the fencing round the Green. And she looked shocked. So all she had to do was give her word and the plans for Baked Bean Alley would be torn up. Triumph. The campaign won.

The trouble was, she wouldn't give her word. I couldn't even get her to talk sense about it.

"It's a bally disgrace," she said to me. "Someone ought to do somethin' about it."

"Exactly, Lady Blitherwicke," I said. "You."

"Me? What can I do?"

"Say no. Say you won't have it."

"Sorry, laddy. One would find oneself on a bit of a sticky wicket if one did that."

"Why? What's stopping you?"

"Gallopin' garters! Look at the time. One's cocoa is brought to one at ten. Mustn't be found to be out, young Demetrius. One must be back in time for one's cocoa."

And she set off in the direction of Blitherwicke Hall. Or she thought she did. In fact she just set off, head down, elbows pumping, little aristocratic legs clicking away like needles. I've never seen anyone so keen to get back for cocoa.

"Lady Blitherwicke," I called, running after her and catching hold of her elbow. "You're heading the wrong way!"

"Oops," she cried and veered round to run off in a different direction. "How's this, laddy? Right this time?"

"More or less but..."

"Don't worry. Once one reaches one's boundary wall one can find one's way to the Hall. Slip in the back way. No one'll ever know. I hope. Be seein' you!"

"But what about Baked Bean Alley?"

"Nice to meet you and all that," she called to me over her shoulder. "Do drop in again some time!"

And she was gone. I stood there for a while open-mouthed and feeling as if my campaign for the Green had just plunged over a cliff. And yet I was sure she was on my side. She really *had* hated the thought of the Green being ploughed up to make an extension for

Turnovers. So what was stopping her doing something about it?

This question puzzled me. In fact, it puzzled me so much that I dreamed about it that night. Lady Blitherwicke and I were in Turnovers. We were penned in by a circle of trolleys and dozens of security men with hats pulled down over their eyes. They were yelling out these fearsome war-cries and Rob was there selling them tins of beans which they lobbed at us like hand-grenades. They made a terrible mess – the place looked as if hundreds of babies had stormed in and been sick. We fought them off with packets of Bobbly-Oddbods which we fired from a catapult made of slinky green tights. Lady Blitherwicke was full of fight in my dream, like Indiana Jones, pinging off biscuits in all directions. Then, quite suddenly, she stopped. A figure in a dark tail-coat with gold buttons pushed its way through the trolleys and Lady Blitherwicke shrank back. She shrank quite literally, in fact, to about knee-height. And shook with fright.

When I woke up, that figure in the dark coat was lodged in my mind. It was Stote, of course. The old lady wasn't afraid of a fight – the way she'd handled her trolley told me that. She was afraid of Stote. But this led to another question. *Why* was she afraid of Stote?

He was a mean old beggar but, surely, if your ancestors fought at Waterloo, you wouldn't be put off by a scrawny butler. Even a bad-tempered one like Stote. There must be something else. But what?

I made my way to the bathroom and, as I washed and dressed, composed a song about it.

Well, I woke up this morning
With an ache in my throat
An' I see in my mind
A nasty old goat
With bright gold buttons
On a long, dark coat
An' a look on his face
Like a dog's behind
But, yeah, it don't scare me
And I just don't mind
'Cause it's Stote,
Only Stote.
Ba-doom, ba-doom,
Yeah, Stote.
Tickety-tickety-tick!
Tickety-ickety-ickety-ickety
Tick.

(That last bit was the drum solo which I beat on the water pipe with my toothbrush.)

"Ivor!"

"Yes, Mum. Just coming."

"I'm getting interference on the Breakfast Weather Report, Ivor. What are you doing up there?"

"Only cleaning my teeth, Mum. I've finished now."

On my way into school I met up with Jessica.

"Hello, Ivor," she said. "How's the nose?"

"The what?"

"The nose. The old man's nose."

"Oh, that. Yes, better, thanks."

"I must say, I was disgusted at the way they treated such an elderly customer. The poor man was terribly confused."

"Quite," I said. "But there you go. That's Turnovers for you."

"It's awful," said Jessica. "I've really gone off them."

"It's the way they do things at Turnovers, though. But I still can't get anyone to listen to my campaign, let alone do anything about it."

"That shouldn't put you off, you know. You shouldn't give up so easily."

"I haven't given up."

"What's the problem, then?"

"I've run up against a brick wall. Called Stote."

"Stote? What's Stote?"

I noticed that she was becoming interested. In fact, she was getting quite fiery about it, her eyes (and her badges) flashing at the thought of battle. So I decided to tell her the story so far, all about the shopping expedition and my worries about Lady Blitherwicke's mysterious butler.

72

"Lady Blitherwicke?" said Jessica, when I'd finished. "You mean that old man was Lady Blitherwicke?"

"Yes."

"But ... but she had a moustache."

"It wasn't real," I explained. "Nor was the nose, for that matter."

"What did she say when you showed her Oak Green?"

"That's the strange thing," I said, as we went in for registration, "she didn't really say anything. She just ran off as soon as I tried to talk about putting a stop to Baked Bean Alley. 'Drop in again,' she says and she's gone."

"Drop in again?"

"Yes."

"Then that's just what we'll do."

"What?"

"Drop in."

"What?"

"We can't leave it like that, Ivor. We've got to go back to Lady Blitherwicke's house and find out what's going on there."

"We"? Who said anything about "we"? But before I could say another word, Mr Makepeace was telling me to sit down and shut up so he could ask me whether I was here or not today.

So it looked as if my one-man campaign had become a two-person campaign, doubling the numbers of the troops in one go. Me and

Jessica. It should've been good news but I wasn't so sure. I know I'd tried to get her interested in the first place but, now she was, I couldn't help remembering the way she always got carried away with her battles against authority. Like dressing up in a sheepskin rug and acting out the agonies of dying lambs on the pavement outside the butcher's shop. If she wanted me to do anything like that, she had another think coming. I believed in more subtle approaches. Protest songs and the like. What Jessica liked was the fight, and sometimes she forgot what she was fighting for.

She said we ought to have a council of war. Five o'clock. The library in town. Well, I thought, I'll turn up, of course, but I shall make quite sure she knows I'm in charge.

11

INTO THE STOTE'S DEN

By six o'clock that evening I was tripping through Lady Blitherwicke's woods, heading for her house. Jessica was leading the way. I don't quite know how this happened. We'd had our council of war and I'd made all the decisions. ("Certainly, Ivor. It's your campaign.") Or, at least, I'd said we weren't going to be doing anything daft or dangerous. ("Of course, Ivor; quite right.") And then she'd suggested that we break into Blitherwicke Hall. And I'd agreed. I suppose. Well, I must've done. ("Good idea, Ivor. Wish I'd thought of it.")

Every now and again Jessica stopped and shushed me.

"Stay on your toes, Ivor," she said. "And don't tread on any twigs. Snapping twigs are a dead giveaway."

"Just a minute," I told her. "Lady Blitherwicke said I could drop in any time. Why do we have to tiptoe through the woods like a couple of pixies?"

"It's obvious, isn't it? If you go swanning up to Lady Blitherwicke's front door, Stote is going to be on his guard. We won't learn anything. Come on. Head down and keep under cover."

After ten minutes or so of nipping from tree to tree and bush to bush, we found ourselves on the edge of a square yard at the back of Blitherwicke Hall. There were three doors facing us and Jessica was all for diving through the nearest one.

"Hang on," I whispered. "Let's try that large one there. By all those bins."

"Why that one?"

"Because I'm sure that one leads to the kitchens, which means it'll probably be unlocked. Besides, I think I can find my way to the rest of the house from there."

"Good thinking, Ivor. Come on."

We dashed across the square and dived for shelter behind the bins where we were almost knocked out by a powerful, rubbishy smell.

"This is awful," gasped Jessica.

"You're telling me. Dead socks and rotten fish."

"No, I mean they throw all their rubbish into the bins without sorting it out first. They ought to separate the glass from the..."

And at that moment we heard someone coming round the side of the house. A crunch of boots on gravel and a thin, tuneless whistle. Then a pause, a throaty cough and a spit. Stote!

"Quick!" I hissed. "He'll find us if we stay here."

We could either dart through the kitchen door and risk bumping into someone else, or take a header into the bins and risk being ponged to death. Without consulting each other, we both made for the door.

The kitchen was dark and for a while we couldn't see a thing. We could hear, though. A woman was singing at the top of her voice.

I'll sing you one-o,
A-peeling of the spuds-o.
One is one and all alone
And in the pot it must go-o!

As my eyes got used to the gloom I saw that it was Mrs Jerkin. She had her back to us and was hacking away at a huge bowl of potatoes. Bits of peel were flying all over the kitchen. As she finished one potato, she lobbed it into the air and headed it into a pot on the stove.

I'll sing you two-o,
A-peeling of the spuds-o.
Two, two and into the ste-EW!

One is one and all alone
And in the pot it must go-o!

This time she juggled the potato on her
plump knee and flicked it in the pot with her
foot.

"Goal!" she cried and punched the air.

She was so engrossed in all this that it was
easy for Jessica and me to edge across the
kitchen and creep up those gloomy steps
which led to the rest of the house. We were
moving slowly, so as not to make a noise, but
the sound of the outer door banging made us
leap up the last three steps in one bound.
Stote's rasping voice interrupted Mrs Jerkin's
song.

"What are you up to now, you turnip?"

Luckily, his eyes had to get used to the
gloom too and I don't think he spotted us. It
was a close call, though, and a couple of
Jessica's badges came rattling off as she slipped
out through the door at the top of the steps.

"Quick," I said. "This way!"

As we hurried along, I tried to remember all
the doors I'd been through the last time I was
in Blitherwicke Hall. Doors to staircases,
bathrooms, libraries and more and more corridors. It wasn't possible to retrace my steps
exactly, because there were people about:
voices and footsteps just out of sight. Sometimes we had to nip down the nearest corridor

or clamber up the closest staircase, just to keep ourselves from being detected. After about five minutes of all this darting about we were well and truly lost.

"I thought you said you knew the way," said Jessica.

"I knew some of the way," I said, "but there's more of it than I remember. Besides, what is the way?"

"The way is where we're going, of course."

"And where are we going?"

"Oh, come on, Ivor. You were at the meeting."

"I know but I can't remember that bit."

"We're going to find Stote's room," said Jessica, beetling off again.

"Hang on a minute. Stote's room? You never said anything about poking around in Stote's room."

"But we have to find his room. How else will we know what he's up to?"

"But, Jessica..."

Too late. She'd gone and I had to skip off after her. We're never going to find Stote's room in a place as big as this, I thought. One poky servant's room out of dozens and dozens? It was impossible.

"Ivor," called Jessica. "I think I've found it."

"What?"

"Come and look at this."

She was standing by a pair of large double

doors which were covered in ornate carvings and decorated in gold-leaf. They were the only doors in a long wide corridor and they obviously opened on to some vast chamber – a ballroom or something.

"Jessica," I said, "we're looking for Stote's room. Stote the butler. He's not going to have a luxurious place like this. He's going to have some hidey-hole at the top of the house…"

She interrupted me with a little cough and pointed to a small sign on one of the doors. "Stote's room," it read. "Keep out."

"Good grief," I said. "You mean Stote lives in here?"

"That's what it says, Ivor. But the doors are locked. You look through the key-hole and see what you can see. I'll keep watch."

I bent down and peered through the key-hole. I could only see a small part of the room but that was enough. The walls were covered with framed oil paintings; there were several comfortable armchairs (all new), a colour TV the size of a small cinema screen, a drinks cabinet, a snooker table, an antique writing desk, a…

"Looking for more biscuits are we, sunshine?"

I jumped up and twirled round. There stood Stote with his arms folded and a sneer on his face. Jessica was nowhere to be seen.

"I … er … hello, there," I mumbled.

"What's the idea?" he snapped.

"I was just … er … passing and I thought I'd pop in to see Lady Blitherwicke…"

"Oh really? Is she in?"

"No. I couldn't see her …"

"What a shame. And was she in the kitchen by any chance?"

"The kitchen?" I swallowed hard. "I … er … haven't been to the kitchen."

"No?" He grinned and unfolded one hand to reveal a small badge. "Befriend a Stray Cat," it said. Stote thrust it under my nose. "Then how did this end up there?"

"I must've dropped it."

"Oh yes, of course. And it rolled down two flights of stairs and through a couple of closed doors to end up on the kitchen steps, I suppose."

"Well, I might've dropped it the last time I was…"

But Stote didn't wait to hear any more. He snaked out an arm and grabbed me by the collar.

"Or are we spying?" he said. "Poking our nose where it doesn't belong?"

I didn't answer. I don't think he wanted an answer. He bundled me through the house while I flailed about in his iron grip, struggling for breath and banging my knees and elbows against the walls and doorknobs and bannisters. When we got to the front door he stood me up, smiling at me with dull yellow teeth and pretending to slap dust from my head and shoulders. Then he placed his finger-tips against my chest and shoved. I tottered, tumbled down the stone steps and ended face down on the gravel drive. The door thudded shut behind me. As I hauled myself up and spat out some small stones, an oily laugh came from the other side of the door.

There was nothing for it but to limp off and count myself lucky to have got away so lightly. If he'd wanted to, Stote could've done worse than just throw me out. After all, I thought, I *was* trespassing. He could've called the police.

I reached the safety of the nearest bush and sat down to dab at my wounds with a hanky. My heart was still pumping with the shock of this sudden attack when I heard a sound close to my left ear.

"Hss!"

Like an angry snake. It was Jessica.

"Don't do that!" I said.

She parted the leaves and sat down beside me.

"Are you all right?" she said.

"Do I look all right? I've got a mouthful of grit and my bones feel like bananas. I'd've been better off hiding in the rubbish bin."

"You've been wounded for the sake of the cause, Ivor. I envy you."

"Thank you very much."

"You can wear those cuts and bruises with pride, you know."

"You could've had a few yourself, Jessica. If only you'd been there when Stote turned up. You *said* you'd keep watch."

"Ah, yes," she said. "I was there, actually, but I'd gone up the corridor and was looking the wrong way at the time. I only just managed to nip round the corner when he turned up."

"Lucky old you."

"It was lucky, really, Ivor. I mean, he *knew* you so he probably wasn't too surprised to find you hanging around. He would've got really suspicious if he'd seen me too. And we don't want that, do we?"

"No, Jessica. I suppose we don't."

"What did you see through the key-hole?"

"Luxury," I said. "Pure luxury. Stote is living like a lord up there."

"Really?"

"Yes. He's supposed to be the butler but he's got that huge room with all that stuff in it and poor old Lady Blitherwicke has a battered old chair and threadbare carpets..."

"Then our mission has been a success," she said. "We have learned something very useful."

"But what? I mean, what does that tell us?"

"It tells us that he must be cheating Lady Blitherwicke or something."

I thought about this for a moment. It didn't

83

sound right to me. If Stote were simply cheating Lady Blitherwicke without her realizing it, he'd keep up the pretence of being a loyal butler. But he didn't. He treated her badly. And she didn't seem to be able to do anything about it.

"I think it's worse than cheating," I said. "She knows he's up to something but she won't do anything about it."

"Or can't."

"Maybe that's it. She can't. She's not being cheated, she's being bullied."

"Or blackmailed, Ivor. Just think about it. Stote caught you snooping around…"

"Yes."

"…but what did he do about it?"

"He biffed me about and threw me downstairs."

"Exactly. He didn't call the police, did he?"

That was true. He didn't call the police. I'd noticed that myself. He didn't even threaten to call the police. Jessica thought that was very significant.

"Come on," she said, jumping up. "We've got to get back. We need to plan the next stage in our campaign."

There was no doubt in her mind: Stote was involved in something suspicious. I was pretty convinced, too. I thought I was, anyway.

Before we made our way back through the woods, I took a last look at the front of

Blitherwicke Hall. It was grey and forbidding in the descending dusk. There were rows of dark windows but only a very few of them were lit. One small one, high up in what I guessed was Lady Blitherwicke's room, and another in the entrance hall where I could see quite clearly a square of cold, lemon light and Stote framed in it, looking out towards the woods. He couldn't see us, though. His mind was on something else. He was nodding slowly and speaking to someone on the phone. Just like you do when you phone the police.

I shuddered and turned away. I don't think I'll tell Jessica about that, I thought.

By the time we got back to town I'd convinced myself that I'd got it all wrong. Stote was bad-tempered and bullying (there was no doubt about that) but he was only doing his best to run the house on behalf of Lady Blitherwicke. I was the one in the wrong. I'd been trespassing, snooping, spying. And Stote *had* phoned the police. He'd seen my letter so he knew where I lived. I half expected to see a car with a flashing blue light parked outside our house.

I pictured myself being thrown in the back of a police van, the neighbours peering at me from behind curtains. And Mum coming to visit me with sandwiches and my pyjamas. Or perhaps not: Mum telling the police that I deserved all I was getting. Prying into the lives of the aristocracy like that. "I tried telling him," she'd sob. "He wouldn't listen. Now he must pay the price for his sin."

Jessica kept chattering about our Plans for the Future. Operation "Stop Stote". We had to be organized. Make badges. Do this, do that. You can't organize much from a prison cell, I thought, and I let her rabbit on without interruption.

"You're very quiet, Ivor," she said at last.

"Am I?"

"You're not losing heart, are you?"

"Well…"

"You mustn't. When right is on your side you have nothing to fear. And right *is* on our side. This man Stote is a villain. He must be stopped."

And at that point we turned into my road and I saw at once that there was no police car outside the house. No peering neighbours, no flashing blue light. And my heart lifted.

"You're right, Jessica," I said. "It's down to us, isn't it?"

"Of course it is. We'll meet again tomorrow morning, then. Operation 'Stop Stote', phase two."

She said goodnight and skipped off, happy as a lamb. I went inside to face Mum: Where do you think you've been? What time do you call this? Why is your face all grazed and your lip swollen, Ivor? Have you been bothering that dear old, blue-blooded Lady again? But I didn't get any of that. She was sitting quietly on the sofa and the telly was off, so I knew something was wrong.

"Mum?" I said. "What's up?"

She looked up at me and I saw that her eyes were red from crying. There was a torn envelope, unstamped, at her feet, and a crisp, cream letter in her hand. As she held it out to me, I recognized the Turnovers name at the top.

"This came through the door ten minutes ago," she said quietly. "We have to get out, Ivor. We've been evicted."

12

BLITHERWICKE HALL REVISITED

I didn't sleep much that night and when I went downstairs in the morning Mum was still sitting on the sofa. I don't think she'd been to bed. She had no idea why the letter had come. I knew, but couldn't tell her.

Jessica turned up bright and early, bristling with ideas. I showed her into the kitchen and told her about the letter while I made some coffee.

"But they can't do it," she said, banging her fist on the table. "This is your home."

"Not any more. Turnovers own it and they say we have to get out."

"Why?"

"They need this place for some of their new employees. The people who'll be working on the new project."

"Baked Bean Alley?"

"Yes. Sickening, isn't it? Here am I trying to stop them taking over the Green and they move in and boot us out of our home."

Jessica chewed her lip and thought.

"Seems a bit of a coincidence," she said. "The very night we discover dark goings-on at Blitherwicke Hall."

"It's not a coincidence at all. When we were leaving last night I saw Stote talking to someone on the phone. At first I thought it was the police, but now I'm sure it's got something to do with that letter."

"You mean he asked someone from Turnovers to sort you out?"

"Yes. And they discovered that they owned the house I lived in. Like they own most of the houses in this street. And the next street. So it was no problem to have us booted out. The perfect solution for them."

"But why should they take any notice of Stote?"

"I wondered that, too. I suppose he said it was Lady Blitherwicke's idea. She owns the place so they thought they ought to jump to it."

"Of course," said Jessica, standing up so suddenly she rocked the table and slopped coffee over it. "Then everything's all right."

"All right? How can everything be all right? We've got a fortnight to clear out. And there's nowhere for us to go."

"You know Lady Blitherwicke, though, don't you?"

"Yes, but..."

"And she likes you, doesn't she? All you have to do is explain all this to her and she'll tell Turnovers to lay off."

"I don't know. Will she?"

"It's worth a try, Ivor. In fact, at the moment, it's the only thing you can do."

So back we went to Blitherwicke Hall. Not tiptoeing round the dustbins this time, but straight in at the front door. Well, almost straight in. We cycled into the grounds and hid the bikes behind a large rhododendron bush at the front of the house.

"Right," said Jessica. "Let's go."

"But what if Stote's on the prowl? It's no good hammering on the front door if he's just going to chuck us straight out again."

She sighed heavily but agreed that it made more sense to keep our eyes skinned and make sure we could speak to Lady Blitherwicke without Stote interfering. For half an hour we hung around the bushes watching for suspicious movements. The house remained absolutely still and silent. Nobody came and nobody went.

"Oh, blow this," said Jessica eventually. "Let's create a diversion. If we can get Stote to chase one of us off, the other one can sneak up to Lady Blitherwicke's room."

"And what happens if he manages to catch you?"

"Me? No, *you* create the diversion and I'll sneak in and..."

"That's no good. You don't know the way. And Lady Blitherwicke doesn't know you."

"But Stote is more likely to go for you..."

"That's what worries me."

"Listen, Ivor. You have to make sacrifices if you want..."

"I have made sacrifices. I've been thrown downstairs and evicted."

Jessica was about to come up with another good reason why I should be the one exposed to danger, when suddenly she froze. Her eyes widened and she clapped a hand to her mouth to stop herself talking. I heard a crunch of tyres on gravel and, through the leaves of a bush, saw a black Bentley sweeping towards us. We flung ourselves down and watched it glide by – away from the house.

"That's Stote at the wheel," I said.

"Come on, then," said Jessica. "Now's our chance!"

We sprinted over the drive and up to the door. It took several minutes before anyone came to answer it. I kept thinking, what if Stote's only gone as far as the main gate? What if he's forgotten something, and comes back and finds us here? Standing at the top of the steps. The very steps he'd thrown me down the night before. Eventually, however, the door creaked open a fraction and a muffled voice asked us what we wanted.

"Is Lady Blitherwicke in?" I said. I felt like a little kid asking if her Ladyship was allowed out to look for conkers or something.

"Who wants her?" the voice wheezed back.

"Ivor Demetrius," said Jessica, loud and clear. "And friend."

The name must've meant something because the door edged open and we stepped into the hall. A deathly white figure stood before us. White from head to foot. Out of the corner of my eye I saw Jessica give a start. It didn't worry me so much because I thought I recognized it.

"I've come from the kitchens," the figure told us. "I'd just measured out the flour when the bell sounded. It made me jump."

"Sorry about that, Mrs Jerkin," I said. "We didn't mean to disturb you."

"That's all right, sonny," said Mrs Jerkin. "Follow me."

She led the way across the hall and padded up the main staircase. Little white clouds puffed into the air with every step she took.

Lady Blitherwicke was delighted to see me again. She sat on the moth-eaten sofa and patted the place beside her. I thought I'd stay on my feet, though. The sofa didn't look strong enough for two.

"You picked a jolly good time to call, young Demetrius," Lady Blitherwicke said. "Stote's out."

"Is he? I didn't realize."

"Who's your chum?" she asked, eyeing Jessica. "Looks a mite familiar."

"Ah," I said. "Perhaps I ought to explain..."

"I'm Jessica," Jessica cut in. Straight to the point. She didn't believe in long explanations. "Don't you remember meeting in Turnovers? I've come to help Ivor keep a roof over his head."

"I say!"

"He's going to be thrown out on to the streets, Lady Blitherwicke."

"Good grief! How bally awful."

"Him and his poor mother. Turned out by Turnovers."

"What?"

"Turnovers. The shop. They own the property and they're kicking Ivor out. It's disgraceful."

"I should say it is. I wouldn't stand for that, young Demetrius."

"Well, Lady Blitherwicke," I began. "The problem is..."

"We're not going to stand for it, Lady Blitherwicke," cut in Jessica again.

93

"Oh good show, Ivor's chum! Make a fight of it. Don't let them push you around." She looked at me with a lop-sided grin. "Bags of spirit this Jessica bird's got. I like that."

"That's why we've come to see you," said Jessica firmly.

"Me?"

"Yes. As owner of Turnovers…"

"What? Owner of who?"

"Turnovers. You own it, Lady Blitherwicke. That's why we're asking you to help."

"Ah."

Lady Blitherwicke got up and walked thoughtfully to the window. She peered through her telescope for a moment, as if she could see some sort of answer to the problem in the far distance.

"Hmm," she said after a while. "Hmm."

"Well?" said Jessica.

"Well?"

"Can you help?"

"One would *love* to help, young Jessica bird," said Lady Blitherwicke, giving the telescope a spin on its tripod and striding back towards us. "Absolutely love to. Especially for a cute sausage like Demetrius here."

She chortled and gave me a playful smack round the back of my head. Jessica was not impressed. She folded her arms and glowered.

"People always say they'd love to help when

they know they're not going to lift a finger," she said.

"The trouble is, old thing, one may own the bally place but that doesn't mean one actually controls it."

"I see." Jessica sighed heavily and turned to me. "We'd better get back, Ivor," she said. "We must sort out some cardboard boxes for you and your poor mother to live in. See if we can find somewhere to put them."

"Oh, I say," said Lady Blitherwicke.

Jessica gave her a withering look and made slowly for the door. Lady Blitherwicke whimpered a little and seemed to crumble. She tugged nervously at the remaining buttons on her cardigan.

"Look here, young Demetrius," she said, "can't you move to your place in the country for a spell?"

"What place in the country?" I asked.

"Haven't you got a little place in Northamptonshire? You could move in there till all this sorts itself out, couldn't you?"

"I'm sorry, Lady Blitherwicke," I said. "I've only got one place..."

"And some rich landowner's about to boot him out of that," put in Jessica.

"Oh pish and tush!" said Lady Blitherwicke. "I won't stand for it. You'll have to believe me when I tell you I can't do a blessed thing about Turnups or whatever the blasted place is called. I really can't. Cross my heart and hope to die in a cellar full of rats. But I will do what I can."

"You will?" twinkled Jessica and the cloud of gloom that had gathered over her head was suddenly no more. She skipped back into the room and took hold of Lady Blitherwicke's hands.

"I knew you wouldn't let us down," she said, plonking a kiss on the old lady's cheek. "You've got such a perky little, kind little face."

That's the trouble with Jessica. One extreme or the other. I was thoroughly embarrassed by all this, but Lady Blitherwicke didn't seem to mind at all.

"Mind you," she said. "There's not much I can do. But young Demetrius and his ailing mater can come and live here."

"What?" I said.

"Not in the house, of course. That would cause all manner of fireworks. No: in the grounds. In the woods, in fact. You can put up a tent or a shed or somethin'."

"Is that it?" said Jessica.

"Best I can do, young bird. The woods are quite splendid in their way, you know. But you must make sure you never, never let Stote find out you're there."

On our way out I had another quick peep

through Stote's key-hole. I didn't really expect to see anything new but the chance seemed too good to miss. My eyes had not deceived me. There was the same collection of luxury goods – the paintings, the chairs, the TV and snooker table. But on the snooker table there *was* something new: a piece of rather interesting evidence.

"Take a look at this, Jessica," I said.

But she wasn't listening. She was still fuming about our interview with Lady Blitherwicke.

"Tight-fisted, miserable old cow," she muttered.

"Jessica, I think you ought to see what Stote's got in there."

"Live in the woods?" she said, storming down the corridor and ignoring my offer to spy through the key-hole. "Is that the best she can do?"

I trotted after her.

"I thought you said she had a kind face."

"I was wrong. She's got a face like a nasty, shifty little snake."

"No she hasn't," I said. "The woods idea was the best she could come up with. But listen. I've just seen…"

"Then she's got a *brain* like a nasty, shifty little snake, too."

Jessica barged out of the house – "Cow!" – and marched over to where we'd left the bikes – "Hard-hearted cow!"

"Don't be too hard on her, Jessica. I think she's too scared to do…"

"Huh! Scared? What's she got to be scared of?"

The answer to this question came in the form of the big black Bentley which turned into the drive at that very moment and sped towards us in a cloud of dust. We were sitting on our bikes right in the middle of the drive, just about to pedal off. No time to dismount. No time to think, even. So we cycled straight back into the rhododendron bush. There was a swishing and a slapping of leaves, a pinging of spokes.

Stote cruised by and, after a second or two of silence, Jessica collapsed backwards out of the bush.

"Pig!" she screeched. "Wrinkly-faced pig!"

She was banging her fists on the ground with frustration. I hauled her to her feet.

"Stinking, rotten pig!"

"Stote, you mean?"

"Of course I mean Stote."

"Well," I said, "it's Stote you should've been blaming all along. Not Lady Blitherwicke."

Jessica ground her teeth and dusted herself down, muttering some more things about cows and pigs which I was glad I didn't quite catch.

"Listen, Ivor," she said when she'd calmed down, "they're both pretty rotten, if you ask me. She won't help you out and he got you in this mess in the first place by pretending to pass on her orders."

"I don't think he did."

"What?"

"I don't think he needed to pass on any message from Lady Blitherwicke," I told her. "He was giving his own orders."

"How do you know that?"

"It's what I've been trying to tell you; what I saw when I was looking through the keyhole."

"What?"

"Plans spread out on the snooker table..."

"Plans?"

"Yes. Plans and a model. A neat little cardboard model of a brand new shop."

"What?"

"Baked Bean Alley."

"In Stote's room?"

"Exactly. In Stote's room, which is kept locked, and which Lady Blitherwicke never goes near."

Jessica stopped fuming for a moment and whistled softly through her teeth.

"You mean Stote's the man behind Baked Bean Alley?" she said.

"I'm sure of it, Jessica," I said. "He's even more powerful than we guessed. Not a cog in a wheel, but the boss. He's the one we're really up against."

13

A ROOF OVER OUR HEADS

We cycled back past Oak Green. It was now chock-a-block with huge yellow diggers, fenced in behind the orange plastic like dozing dinosaurs. The thing that disturbed me most, though, was the sight of a chainsaw propped up against the oak itself. J. Britch, the rat-faced man, was there again, busily knocking a notice into the ground. When he saw us wheeling our bikes towards him, he stopped hammering and gave us a ratty snarl.

"Shove off, kiddies," he said.

"We have every right to be here," Jessica told him and he raised his eyebrows and curled his lips at her.

"You have only one right as far as I'm concerned, girlie," he said, "and that's the right to shove off."

Jessica wasn't put off by that. She smiled sweetly at him and stayed where she was. He scowled and went back to bashing his notice, hitting it as if he hoped it would hurt.

The notice read:

By public demand
BAKED BEAN ALLEY
An exciting new extension to
the Turnovers concept
Work starts on
MONDAY JULY 4th

"That's just over a week," I said. "We'll never stop them in that time."

"Stop us?" chortled Britch. "Stop us? A couple of kiddies? That's a good one. That really is."

"It will be a good one," said Jessica, "when you're sent packing."

He was still gurgling with laughter when we cycled off.

The rest of the weekend was dismal. Grey. Flat. Hopeless. I felt listless and fed up. Mum couldn't bring herself to leave the house. She said she wasn't sure it would still be there when she got back. So she moped about the place, picking up Princess Di mugs from time to time and fondling them.

"Where am I going to put them, Ivor?" she

sniffed. "This is their home. It's where they belong."

"Don't worry, Mum," I said. "We'll find somewhere."

"But where? I can't go just anywhere, you know."

"Well … I have had an offer as a matter of fact."

I hadn't planned to tell her about it. I didn't think she'd take too kindly to camping out in the woods. Nowhere to display the mugs, and nowhere to plug in the telly. Still, she sounded so worried I felt I had to say something.

"Woods, Ivor?" she said. "What do you take me for? A squirrel? I cannot possibly doss down in some mucky old wood."

"It won't be any old wood, Mum. It'll be a special wood."

"A wood is a wood is a wood," she said gravely. "I refuse to make my home with wolves and vultures."

Wolves and vultures? She'd been watching too much David Attenborough. Or not enough, maybe.

"Listen, Mum, I've been back to see Lady Blitherwicke…"

"Don't make things worse, Ivor. Please. It's bad enough being made homeless without hearing horrible tales of you belching and burping in the homes of the landed gentry. I'm just not up to it."

"I didn't belch or burp…"

"I should hope not."

"But I did tell Lady Blitherwicke about being evicted…"

"You didn't! Oh the shame of it."

"And she said we could move in there."

"WHAT?"

"Well, not into Blitherwicke Hall exactly. Into the grounds."

"Lady Blitherwicke's grounds?"

"Yes."

"You mean these woods you've been going on about are Lady Blitherwicke's woods?" she asked, her voice rising to a squeak.

"Well … yes."

"Oh, Ivor. What an honour. Me, on noble soil. By permission of a real Lady…"

"You won't mind, then?"

"Mind? Why should I mind? How many other people do you know who can say they live in noble woods?"

"What about the Princess Di mugs?"

"I'll hang them from Lady Blitherwicke's twigs and things. It'll be the perfect setting for them."

So at least I was able to cheer Mum up. For myself, though, I couldn't be quite so enthusiastic. I didn't see it the way Mum did. The way I saw it, we'd be stretched out under the stars with Lady Blitherwicke's pigeons dropping nasty things on our homeless heads.

Thank goodness it was summer.

On the Monday of half-term week Jessica came round to help plan the next campaign move. At least, we tried to plan, sitting at the kitchen table for ages and staring at a blank notebook, but we didn't get anywhere. We simply had no idea what to do next.

"We must do something," Jessica said.

"What, though? Everything we've tried so far has only made things worse."

"Why don't we chain ourselves to the bulldozers?" she suggested.

"Because it won't work, Jessica."

"It might."

"It won't. They'll plough us in and say they never noticed us. Rat-face would just love that. And don't say we have to make sacrifices because there's no point making sacrifices if it means being squashed into the mud and Baked Bean Alley still being built. On top of us."

"Still," said Jessica, "it is half-term and that gives us a lot more time."

But all the time in the world is no good to you if you don't know what to do with it. So we ended up mooching around, heaving sighs and fiddle-faddling about. Getting nowhere very, very slowly. Jessica made some "Turnovers Are Tyrants" badges and I composed a new song.

Well I ain't got nowhere
To lay down my weary head.
No I ain't got nowhere
To lay down my poor weary head.
And I ain't got no roof
And I ain't got no comfy bed.
Well I ain't got no...

"Ivor. Do you mind?" said Jessica a minute or two after I'd started.

"What?"

"That's awful. It's just making me miserable."

"Well, it's supposed to be sad. It's a blues number..."

"I mean it *sounds* so dismal. It's not proper singing and it's ungrammatical."

"What?"

"It should be 'I haven't got any' not 'I ain't got no.'"

"I can't sing that."

"You can't sing at all, Ivor."

"Oh thanks very much. I'm just supposed to bottle it all up, am I?"

"I would prefer it, yes."

And that was the end of my song. I'm discovering that it's best to do what Jessica wants.

In the afternoon I went for a walk. Walking is good for getting ideas to flow, I always find.

This time, though, all my thoughts drifted down the same two dead-ends: Mum and I had nowhere to live, and the Green was still going to be turned into Baked Bean Alley. But when I got back I discovered that an interesting development had taken place.

I heard Mum singing "Land of Hope and Glory" in the kitchen. If Jessica is right about my singing, I know where I get my voice from. The singing wasn't the interesting development, though. A delivery van had brought that.

I let myself in, flung open the door to the kitchen and walked in. Not into the kitchen but into a wall of solid wood. I bounced back into the hall and blinked at it. What was a wall of solid wood doing inside our kitchen? For a moment I thought the eviction had already started and this was something unpleasant to do with Turnovers.

"Ivor," came Mum's voice from the other side of the wall. "Is that you?"

"Yes," I said. "I can't get in. What's going on?"

"Open the door."

"I have opened the door."

"Not that door. The other door. The door in front of you."

When I looked more closely I could see that the wall of wood had a handle to it. I turned it, it opened and I peered cautiously into the kitchen. Mum was sitting at the table with a mug of tea.

"Would you like tea?" she said. "It's not very old."

"Why have we got two doors to our kitchen, Mum? Those double-glazing people haven't been round again, have they?"

"Of course not. This is the shed."

"Shed? What shed?"

"The shed we're going to live in in Lady Blitherwicke's woods. Isn't it lovely?"

I turned round and saw a length of wooden wall propped against the kitchen door. It had a red stamp on it: Trends of the Earth.

"But ... but is this it?" I said.

"Well, this is a bit of it. It wouldn't all fit in the kitchen."

"Where's the rest?"

She pointed to the back room.

"In there on the floor is the roof, and the sides are in the front and the back's round the side."

"Pardon?"

"The roof's in there, on the back room floor. The sides are in the front room and they've put the back outside. Round the side."

"I see. Where did it come from?"

"Some very nice men brought it round from Trends of the Earth. I told them they must've made a mistake but they said they hadn't. They'd been told to deliver it and they gave me

107

a little note in an envelope. Where is it now?"

She went into the back room where the shed roof was covering most of the floor, edged round to the front room which she entered by clambering over a pile of chairs. Two wooden walls, with windows in them, faced each other across the room. One was leaning against the fireplace and the other against the front window. Ours is a very small house: it's a miracle they got the shed in at all.

"It's a wee bit inconvenient at the moment," said Mum. "I have to stand on the sofa and watch the telly through this little window. But it won't be for long, will it? Ah, here we are."

She found an envelope pinned to one of the walls, and handed it to me. Inside was a white card with gold edging and scrawled on it were the words, *With compliments, M.B. P.S. don't tell S.* It took me a second or two to work out that "M.B." was Marigold Blitherwicke and "S." – well, of course, it was obvious who "S." was.

I was quite touched that the old lady had gone to so much trouble. It couldn't have been easy to arrange without letting Stote know. A bit risky, even. And expensive. Jessica could hardly call her a mean old cow now.

"I think it's going to be ever so cosy, Ivor, don't you?" said Mum.

"Oh yes, Mum," I said. "Lovely."

Just then we heard a tapping sound which

we weren't able to trace for some moments. At first we thought it was coming from the television but it sounded too lively for that.

"It's the window, Ivor," said Mum eventually. "There's someone tapping at the window."

And there was. I had to crawl round the side of the shed and inch my way along the skirting before I could trace the source of the sound.

A small, pinched face was staring at me from the street. A man's face. It was narrow and pale with a dark, drooping moustache. And it was topped by a bowler hat. In fact, the way that the bowler hat was pulled down tight to the eyebrows, so that you could hardly see the man's eyes at all, reminded me of someone I thought I knew. But I couldn't think who for the moment.

The man looked at me without smiling and continued to tap on the window with the handle of his umbrella.

"I'm from Sheds and Shelters (Regulations Division)," he mouthed through the glass.

I signalled that I would let him in at the front door and he nodded gravely. Then I crawled backwards, edging myself along on both elbows, till I found myself in the hall.

"Do come through," I said to the man and I led him back into the front room – the long way round – through both the kitchen door and the solid wood, round the roof, over the chairs and into a space between the propped up sides of the shed. We had to stand nose to nose, almost, and I didn't like the look of him. I don't think Mum did either.

"I'm from Sheds and Shelters (Regulations Division)," he repeated when it was clear we were going no further.

"Really?" said Mum. "That must be interesting work. Would you like some tea?"

"Not while I'm on duty, thank you," he said. Then, fixing her with a fierce and steady gaze, he asked, "Have you, by any chance, just purchased a shed, madam?"

"No," she said. "I don't think so."

The man in the hat gave a little start and looked round the room.

"Then what, pray, is this, madam?" he asked, tapping the nearest bit of shed with the end of his umbrella.

"Ah, that," smiled Mum. "Of course, *that* shed. Well, I haven't exactly bought it..."

"No, but it is ours," I cut in. "All legal and above board."

The man looked at me sharply and placed a small cross on a clip-board.

"Would I be correct in assuming that it is a *garden* shed, madam?" he continued.

"I expect so."

"Then why, pray, is it not in the garden?"

"It's too big," I said.

"So what do you plan to do with it?"

Mum and I exchanged glances.

110

"Well," she said, "we could put it up in here, I suppose..."

"Tch, tch, tch. Sorry," said the man. "You can't put a shed up indoors. Against regulations. Against several regulations, as a matter of fact."

"Oh."

"In fact, the only place you can put up a garden shed round here is in the garden."

"This shed would completely cover our garden, though," I said.

"Then you can't do that either," he declared, making several more neat crosses on his clipboard. "If your garden is completely covered it is no longer a garden. It is a spare room. And spare rooms are..."

"Against the regulations?" asked Mum.

"Yes."

"I thought so. Well, I promise I won't use it in the garden and I won't put it up in here either..."

"Then what, pray, are you going to do with it?"

"We're going to sleep in it," she said with a smile.

The man turned so suddenly red that I thought the hat was going to shoot off the top of his head.

"Sleep in it? Good heavens, no. You can't sleep in a garden shed, madam. That's against so many regulations it would take me all day to explain them to you. I would have to be down on you like a ton of bricks if you did a thing like that, madam."

"But suppose it was in the garden, and it wasn't too big, and I went in it and fell asleep by accident?" asked Mum. "What about that?"

"You would be contravening By-law 387b, subsection 17 (the use of sheds, 1979). And I would still be down on you like a ton of bricks, madam."

"But how would you know?"

"I'd know all right, madam. I have ways of knowing what goes on in sheds."

He moved even closer to Mum, so close that the rim of his bowler was almost touching her nose.

"Haven't you heard of the Hermon Hill Shed Squad, madam?"

"No. Who are they?"

"The Hermon Hill Shed Squad is me and my brother. We keep tabs on every shed in the area. Make sure people stick to the regulations."

"And who are you?"

The man handed her a small card. It said:

Sheds and Shelters (Regulations Division):
G. Trussett (Inspector).

"I am G. Trussett," he said. "The G. stands for Gisborn. My brother is Rupert Trussett. He helps me during the day. In the evenings I help him. He works in Security at Turnovers."

"I think I know him," I said.

"Then you'll know what I mean when I refer to tons of bricks, lad," said Gisborn Trussett. "Right. I must be off. Just a friendly call, madam. To let you know we're on to you, madam. If you do plan any funny business with this shed, the Shed Squad will know all about it. Goodbye, madam. Have a nice day."

He gave a little nod, climbed back over the chairs and was gone. Mum and I were left looking at each other and feeling a bit trembly. After all, we had just been given a pretty heavy warning. There was no doubt about that. Nothing would've pleased the Trussetts more than to catch us breaking one of those endless, petty regulations. And we knew what that would mean. A ton of Turnovers bricks. I could see them raining down on us from a great height, tipped by the smiling Trussett brothers and, I was perfectly sure, a grinning Stote. I didn't know how Stote had heard about our shed almost before we had. But he must've done, somehow. It was no coincidence that Gisborn Trussett had turned up only an hour or two after the delivery.

"Ivor," said Mum quietly, "the sooner we can get this shed on to Lady Blitherwicke's noble soil, the better, I think."

And I had to agree with her.

14

FLITTING

By Tuesday morning Jessica had regained her spirits. We met in town for our next planning session.

"I can't think in your house," she told me. "It's too muddly."

She was waiting for me outside the library at nine-thirty, hopping from foot to foot with impatience.

"Where have you *been*?" she said. "I've been standing around here for ten minutes."

"It's not so easy to get in and out of the kitchen these days," I said. "Bits of shed all over the place..."

"Oh yes."

"We've got to get that shed out to Blitherwicke Hall. Fast."

"Oh pooh," said Jessica. "That's no problem. We can put it in my dad's van."

"I didn't know your dad had a van."

"Of course he's got a van. How do you transport fish without a van?"

"I didn't know he transported fish."

"Of course he does. But we have more pressing problems than shed-shifting, Ivor. We've got to tackle Turnovers before next Monday."

"I know," I sighed. "But we've been through all that. Turnovers are ahead of us at every step..."

"Agreed. It's no good taking on the whole lot of them. We have to break down a single person, not an organization."

"Stote, you mean?"

"No."

"We won't get anywhere with him."

"Not Stote, Ivor. Lady Blitherwicke."

"But Lady Blitherwicke has no power.."

"Ah. Why not, though?"

"Because of Stote. It all comes back to Stote."

"Quite. Lady Blitherwicke can't do anything about Baked Bean Alley because Stote has her in his power. And why does Stote have her in his power?"

"I don't know," I said. I was beginning to think all this was going round in circles.

"Nor do I. But, if we did know, we might be able to do something about it."

"So..."

"So the next thing we have to do is ask Lady Blitherwicke what Stote is up to."

Well, it made sense but I couldn't see it working. Were we supposed to swan into the old lady's room and ask her straight out: why has your butler got you in his power? I didn't think she'd tell us much. On the other hand, as Jessica pointed out, there wasn't much else we could do.

"Tell you what," she said. "We'll move you into the woods tonight. That'll give us the chance to sneak off and have another little chat with Lady Blitherwicke."

Jessica's dad's van rolled up outside our house at about eight-thirty that evening. We thought it was best to make it that late so that we could sneak the shed into the grounds of Blitherwicke Hall as it was getting dark.

"Come on, team," said Jessica in high spirits. "Let's shift this shed."

We hauled the sections into the back of the van and then bundled some bedding, a few bits and pieces and Mum in after it. The rest we'd have to take some other time. Mum was quite excited at the thought of the move. She sat on a pile of blankets, wedged in between the shed roof and the side of the van, and talked the whole time.

"We're doing a flit," she said. "A moonlight flit. I've always wanted to do a flit. It's sort of

116

romantic, isn't it? And, of course, we're flitting to a far, far better place than the one we're leaving. Don't you think, Ivor? Jessica? There's a very interesting aroma in the back of this van, I must say…"

"That's because it's a fish van," said Jessica's dad. And he clunked the doors shut.

That was almost the only thing he said all night. He was short, like Jessica, but as slow and silent as she was lively and chatty. I suppose he didn't get much chance to join in conversations at home. He wore a brown overall, stained with fish oil and buttoned tight across his chubby chest. I couldn't work out whether he minded being dragged out at night to help us. He didn't look as if he minded, but he didn't look as if he were finding it a lot of fun either. He sat behind the wheel of the van, a pipe clamped between his teeth, and drove off in silence.

It was dark by the time we reached Blitherwicke Hall. A deep, rich, countryside dark. The van bobbed along, the pool of its headlights following the high wall of the estate, until we came to the main gates. Which were shut and locked. Jessica's dad switched off the engine and swung out of the cab. We clambered out after him and stood there hopelessly.

"Oh no," said Jessica. "Didn't you know the gates would be locked?"

"I didn't think about them," I said.

"Well, maybe you should've done, instead of droning out those awful songs."

"You didn't think about them either," I pointed out.

She walked up to the gates and pushed. They clanked but remained shut. Her dad settled himself on the front bumper of the van and relit his pipe.

"We've stopped," came Mum's voice from the back of the van. "Why have we stopped?"

I opened the doors and let her out. An aroma of fresh wood and stale fish wafted into the night air. As soon as she saw the gates her face fell.

"We can't get in, Ivor," she said. "The gates are locked."

"I know."

"Then we'll have to phone Lady Blither-wicke and ask her to send someone to open them…"

"No, Mum. We can't do that."

"Well, how else are we going to get in?"

"We can't get in, Mrs Demetrius," said Jessica. "Pavarotti here forgot to arrange it."

"Now listen," I said. "It wasn't entirely my fault…"

Jessica's dad stood up quickly and took his pipe out of his mouth. This sudden movement came as such a surprise that we all fell silent and looked at him.

118

Flitting

"There's someone coming," he mumbled.

A quick, light crunching of gravel on the other side of the gates. A shadowy form darting towards us between a line of trees.

"Right," hissed Jessica. "We've broken down. We don't know where we are."

"But we do," said Mum. "We're outside Blitherwicke Hall and…"

"Ssh," said Jessica, lifting the bonnet and leaning into the engine as if in the middle of fiddling with some vital nut or bolt. "Ivor, you mustn't be seen. Get round the side."

I hurried round the side and leaned against the van, holding my breath. My ears were tuned to the slightest sound.

"I say," came a familiar voice. "Can't see a bally thing. Who is it out there?"

I heaved a sigh of relief and ran back from my hiding place.

"It's me," I said. "Ivor. We've got the shed."

"Oh, good show," said Lady Blitherwicke, her pale face pressed against the iron railings. "Thought it might be you. Came down here last night but there was no sign. Half a mo'. One had the wretched key here a moment ago."

She produced a huge key and Jessica and I helped her swing the gates open. The van drove slowly in, followed by Mum who fell to her knees as soon as she crossed on to Lady Blitherwicke's land.

"I've arrived," she said and kissed the drive. "I have actually set foot on noble soil."

It wasn't easy putting the shed together in the dark. We had to work in the thick of the woods, between awkward tree trunks and overhanging branches. It would've been no good building the thing in an open space that could be seen clearly from the house when morning came. There was a lot of muttering and straining and bodies getting in the way of other bodies.

Eventually, however, the shed began to take shape and we stood back so that Jessica's dad could put the finishing touches.

"I say," whispered Lady Blitherwicke, "it's nearly cocoa time. One had better scoot."

"But the shed's nearly finished," said Jessica. "Can't you stay to see them in their new home?"

"Sorry, young bird. Cocoa calls."

"Oh no, Lady Blitherwicke. It's not really cocoa calling, is it?"

"Isn't it?"

"No. It's Stote. You're afraid that Stote will find your room empty and come looking for you."

"Well, he's an evil-tempered curmudgeon, is Stote," said Lady Blitherwicke nervously. "Butlers often are, you know."

"That doesn't mean you have to be afraid of them."

"Afraid? Blitherwickes don't know the meanin' of fear, my girl."

"You must be afraid," Jessica pressed on. "You let him boss you around and you don't stand up to him and..."

"It's not because one is afraid. Not afraid for oneself, you understand..."

"Then why is it?"

"Well..."

"Yes?"

"I'll tell you but you mustn't breathe a word to anyone about this."

A patch of moonlight fell on Jessica's face, which was wide-eyed and innocent, like a sweet little thing waiting for a bedtime story. I don't know whether the look was natural or whether she was able to switch it on at will, but I have my suspicions.

"We won't say a word, will we, Ivor?" she said. "But if we knew what Stote was up to we might be able to help."

"Oh, I don't think so, bird. You see, for many years Stote was butler to my old pater, Lord Armitage. I never liked the man. Stote, I mean. When Pater passed away I decided it was time to find a new butler. I summoned Stote up to my rooms and in he came, grinnin' like a blessed cod-fish, but when I started talkin' about findin' a new post and wot-not, the bally blighter helped himself to the cigars and simply smirked."

"Smirked?"

"Smirked. What sauce! 'Now, look here, Stote,' I said. 'No,' he said. 'You look here. When the old boy popped off, I had the good fortune to lay my hands on a pretty little book he kept by the side of his bed. And you know what that was, don't you?'"

"Did you?" I asked.

"Unfortunately I did, young Demetrius. It was Pater's diary. 'Now you wouldn't want a thing like that to fall into the wrong hands, would you, Lady B?' he said. 'What with it being full of such horrible, dark secrets and all.' The bounder!"

"But was it?" said Jessica. "Full of dark secrets, I mean."

"I don't know, Jessica bird. They were secret, you see. Pater never said a word to me about them. But I couldn't risk it. After all, if someone told you your parent had done some extremely silly things, would you believe them? Would you risk tellin' that person to buzz off?"

Jessica and I looked at each other and thought for a moment. It was very easy to believe that parents had done a whole string of stupid things in the past. I only hoped that Mum didn't keep a diary.

"So," went on Lady Blitherwicke, "I had to preserve the good name of the Blitherwickes and that meant doin' exactly what Stote told me to do."

"Just as we thought," said Jessica. "Blackmail."

"That's the truth of the matter, I'm afraid. Stote is the real master of Blitherwicke Hall and one can't do a bally thing about it while he has the diary in his possession."

"Right, Lady Blitherwicke," said Jessica with determination. "You'd better get back to your room. But don't worry. Now we know what the problem is we'll be able to do something about it. Won't we, Ivor?"

"Oh yes," I said. "Yes. Of course."

"You're a couple of true cheeses, you two," muttered Lady Blitherwicke, and she blew her nose. She was much moved by Jessica's words. "I'm sure you won't be able to put one over on Stote but I'm most touched by what you say. Most touched."

She gave us each a hearty slap round the back of the head and set off for the house. Great, I thought. Now we know *why* Stote has her under his thumb. But what are we going to do about it? Jessica had made it sound as if there'd be no problem. But what on earth could we *do*? That's what I wanted to know.

15

EMERGENCY MEASURES

Living in the woods wasn't at all like I thought it was going to be. For a start, although it was summer, the nights were cold. And then it took so long to do things. Boiling a kettle and cooking over a fire, for example. Even starting the fire in the first place.

Still, Mum loved it. And we were safer in the thick of the trees than we had been back at home with men from Turnovers and the Council (Sheds and Shelters) snooping around. Or so I thought. In the early light of our first morning, the shed looked exposed and obvious. You couldn't see it from the house but, if you decided to take a stroll through the woods, you might easily stumble across it. Of course, Stote wasn't the sort to take strolls, but you never know with a criminal mind like his. Better to be prepared.

So, while Mum arranged her mugs and toiled over a feeble fire, I spent a couple of hours fiddling around with some fallen branches and a length of rope Jessica's dad had left us. I was making what I called my Emergency Measures: a clever device to protect the shed from prying eyes. If the need should arise.

I explained it all to Mum but she just smiled and told me to gather dry sticks for the fire.

"Nothing boils on this thing," she said. "What I need is a good blaze, Ivor."

So off I went to look for kindling. In spite of my worries about the shed being easy to spot, I didn't expect to meet anyone. The odd squirrel or one of Lady Blitherwicke's deer, perhaps. Certainly not an old man on his hands and knees, crawling over the forest floor in a darting fashion more like a crab than anything. His back was straight and his woolly hat was pulled down till it almost covered his eyes.

"Have you lost something?" I asked him.

The old man leapt to his feet and spun round twice before he noticed me. He looked even more strange standing up. He was wearing two or three overcoats, dark glasses and, on one side of his face only, a white beard.

"What?" he snapped. "What are you after?"

"Can I help? Have you lost anything?"

"Oh, yes, yes," he said, suddenly bending

double and clutching his back. "I can't quite find my way."

His voice was now wavery with age, and he really did look quite old. Except that his beard was still sticking out of the side of his face.

"I usually cut through these woods, little boy, and I know I'm on the right track when I see a wooden hut – a shed, you might say – among the trees somewhere. You haven't by any chance seen one, have you?"

Oh no, I thought. Surely not. Not already.

"Oh yes," I told the old man. "I know just what you mean. Follow me."

And I led him through the woods at a steady pace, leaping ditches and ducking under branches.

"Are we nearly there?" the old man kept asking.

But, of course, we weren't. We were no nearer to the shed than we'd been when we started. In fact, I was taking him everywhere in the woods *except* where the shed was.

"Stop, stop," the man said at last, leaning against a tree for breath. "We must be nearly there now."

"I *thought* we should be," I said, "but I must've made a mistake. Perhaps there isn't a shed in the woods after all. Sorry."

"Sorry?" breathed the man. "Sorry? You will be sorry, you haddock. You know very well there *is* a shed in these woods and you live in it. Now where is it?"

"I don't know what you're talking about, Mr Trussett," I said.

"What? Trussett? Why are you calling me that? I'm not Trussett. I'm a poor old man with a long white beard..."

"Growing on the back of your head?"

Because that's where the beard was by this time. Trussett fingered his chin and found nothing there.

"Blast!" he said.

He began to flail his arms about and pull various coats and scarves off. It was no surprise to me to see a Trussett emerging from this scrum, although I wasn't sure whether it would be Rupert (of Turnovers Security) or Gisborn (of Sheds and Shelters). As this one wore a blue uniform beneath all his overcoats I knew it was Rupert.

"Right!" he said, still struggling out of his disguise. "If this is the way you want it – puff-urgh-nnff – this is the way you'll – argh-gerroff – get it!"

But I was much too quick for him. Trussett grumbled and stumbled after me. I nipped in and out of trees and swung along until the only sign of Trussett was an angry voice in the distance.

"Haddock! You young haddock ... just you wait..."

Getting fainter and fainter.

It was annoying to think they were on to us already but I was pleased with the way I'd been able to get rid of him. Easy, I thought. Almost too easy. They're townies, those Trussetts, not used to moving through the wild.

But when I got back to the shed with my bundle of kindling, I saw something which made me stop in my tracks.

There, peering in through the window, was an old man with a white beard.

At first I thought it was Rupert Trussett again. Perhaps he'd stumbled on a short cut and found what he was looking for after all.

"Can I help you?" I asked, cautiously.

The old man leapt in the air and twisted round in one movement, collapsing backwards against the shed.

"Arrgh!"

But his beard stayed on his chin.

"Oh ah," he said when he'd recovered his breath. "Could you be a-tellin' an old feller all about this 'ere shed, moi young laddie-o. On account of Oi've never seed it 'ere afore an' it do fair intrigue me. Oh ah, oh ah."

It couldn't be a real old man. Not talking like that. It was the *other* Trussett. Gisborn, the shed inspector himself.

"Shed?" I said. "What shed?"

"Oh ah, moi fair young laddie-o," mumbled

Gisborn. "This 'ere shed 'ere, me old pal, me old beauty."

"I see no shed."

Gisborn blinked. He looked from me to the shed and back.

"This 'ere shed 'ere," he repeated with a twitch of his head.

"A shed?" I said, smiling with great interest. And beginning to wander away. "You mean one of those little furry ones with the fluffed out tails?"

"What? No, no. That's a squirrel."

"Ah, of course. A squirrel. Yes, I've seen a good few squirrels about."

"Yes, but…"

"Was there any one in particular you wanted to know about?"

"No," said Gisborn with a snort. His funny voice had gone by now. From the depths of his grubby overcoat he had produced a notebook and he was following me closely, licking the point of a pencil.

"No," he said, "there isn't a particular squirrel I want to know about at all."

"Just any old squirrel?"

"No, no. Not a squirrel. A shed! That shed back there!"

"A shed? Hmm. You've got me a bit stuck there, I'm afraid."

"A shed, you dim pudding! A shed, a shed, a shed!"

"Bless you."

We were now fifty metres or so from the shed, trotting down a leafy slope into a little hollow. That's two Trussetts disposed of, I thought. But I thought too soon because Gisborn suddenly lost patience and grabbed me by the collar.

"I've had enough of this," he said. "Don't try to tell me you don't know what a shed is because I won't believe it. I'm too sharp for a trick like that. Sharp and quick was always my watchword!"

"That's three words."

"And cut out the clever dick comments, sonny. You know what I'm after and you know what a shed is, right?"

"I think so," I said.

"Right. So tell me."

"A shed is a creature which scampers about in the trees. It has little front paws like hands and..."

"No, no, no," screeched Gisborn and I thought he was going to bang his head against a tree. Or, more likely, bang mine. "It hasn't got paws, clod-bonce! It's made of wood!"

"Wood?"

"Thick, solid planks of wood."

"Then how can it bury nuts?"

And that was the last straw. He dragged me out of the hollow, up the little slope and back through the trees towards the shed.

"LOOK!" he said. "THAT IS A SHED, YOU USELESS, DOZY ANIMAL! A SHED!! UNDERSTAND?"

He waved his clenched fist over his shoulder in the direction of the shed.

But when he turned round, the shed wasn't there. It had scampered off.

Gisborn was so stunned by what he saw – or rather, by what he didn't see – that his mouth dropped open and he let go of me. I scrambled to my feet and ran off.

"Where did it go?" I heard him ask himself. "Where *did* it go?"

But he was unable to answer. There was no one around to answer for him either: I was well out of the way by then.

So, where *had* the shed gone?

This brings me back to my Emergency Measures. The device was quite simple, really. A screen of shrubs, bushes, branches and twigs suspended from the nearest tree. Someone had only to tug on a rope and the whole lot would swing down and fall into place, obscuring the shed. If you looked hard you'd still be able to see it, but Gisborn Trussett had been in no mood for calm, careful observation.

I gave him the run-around for ten minutes and then doubled back to find Mum poking at her dwindling fire.

"Did you get the sticks, Ivor?" she said.

"Because there'll be no tea till I get a few flames out of this thing."

"You did it, Mum. You activated the Emergency Measures."

"What? Pulled the rope, you mean? Of course I did. That's what you told me to do, isn't it?"

"Well yes but…"

"So I did it. Has that funny old man gone? I thought he was a bit suspicious myself. You shouldn't talk to funny old men, Ivor. Now, what about these sticks?"

16

BREAK-IN

Jessica joined us in the afternoon. She came trundling through the trees with her bike and dropped it against the shed.

"You'll never guess what I've just seen outside the gates," she said as she fell to the ground by Mum's fire. "Two funny old men with hats pulled down over their eyes..."

"And long white beards," I said.

"And long white beards, yes. And what do you think they were doing?"

"Arguing?"

"More than arguing, Ivor. They were fighting. Rolling about in the grass and trying to clobber each other senseless."

"Gisborn and Rupert Trussett. They've been looking for the shed."

"Already?"

"Yes. Stote knows we're up to something.

He must've tipped them off."

"So why were they fighting?"

"Probably because they're blaming each other for failing to find us. But it won't take them long to be back for another go."

Mum poured some tea into a couple of Fergie mugs and handed them to us. The tea was cool and white, with tea-leaves and insects floating on its surface.

"Well, at least we've got the Emergency Measures," she said.

"We can't keep using the Emergency Measures, Mum."

"Why not?"

"Well ... because."

"Because what?"

"Because they're for emergencies, that's why."

"What if we keep getting emergencies, though?" asked Jessica.

"We still can't use them. It takes hours to set up all those ropes and things."

"Then don't set them up. Leave them down. They more or less cover the shed, don't they?"

"Yes, but the point of having a moving screen is that you can confuse the enemy. Sometimes the screen's there and sometimes it's not..."

"And when it's there," said Jessica as if explaining kerb drill to a puppy, "the enemy can't see the shed, but when it's not there they *can*."

She had a point. I realized that; but it had taken me ages to rig the screen up so that it could move and I didn't want to abandon the idea just like that.

"I know what we should do," said Mum suddenly. "Patrol the woods."

"We can't do that either," I said.

"Why not?"

"Because if we march around watching for Inspectors of Sheds and Shelters all day, we won't be able to do anything about Stote. He'll go ahead with his plans for Baked Bean Alley without anyone to stop him."

"Still," said Mum, sipping daintily at her cold tea, "I don't suppose those silly old men'll be back just yet. And the shed is well hidden at the moment, isn't it?"

"Very well hidden," said Jessica. "It took me ages to find it and *I* knew where it was."

"Which gives us a bit of time, doesn't it?"

"Well, yes, I suppose so," I agreed. "We're safe from attack at the moment."

Just then something burst in on us with a violent rustling of leaves and crashing of twigs. It moved so quickly I couldn't make out what it was. Except that it had wheels and made a terrible wailing sound. It shot through the middle of the fire, knocking the kettle hissing into the ash and scattering Fergie mugs all over the place. Then it ran into the side of the shed with a clunk. I wasn't sure whether to do battle with it or to turn and run. For a second there was silence. Then the thing groaned.

"Well, give us a bally hand," it said. "I've got my cardie caught in this perishin' chain."

It was Lady Blitherwicke. On a bike.

We managed to untangle her from the chain and sit her down by the remains of the fire. Mum rescued one of the mugs and brought her some tea.

"I say, old horse," said Lady Blitherwicke. "Plenteous thanks."

Mum was too nervous to say anything: she just made a deep curtsy and walked away backwards till she was stopped by a tree.

Lady Blitherwicke sipped once at the tea, glanced down suddenly at it before grimacing and tossing it on to the ashes.

"Thought you'd all cleared orf," she told us. "Couldn't find sight nor sign of you anywhere. Traipsin' about all mornin' and gettin' nowhere. Went back to borrow Jerkin's cycle-machine."

"We're not so easy to find, Lady Blitherwicke," said Jessica. "Ivor built a screen."

"I know that now, young bird. I've just come through it." She gave Mrs Jerkin's bike a withering look. "Thanks to that wretched thing. It's a danger to life, that is. Sends one shootin' into the woods whether one wants to go there or not."

"You didn't know we were here, then?" I asked.

"Not until I came through your devilish screen, young sausage. Pure chance, really. Still, now I'm here I'd better tell you what I know. There's been goin's-on up at the Hall. Weird old beggars with beards wanderin' about..."

"We've seen them," I said.

"Have you, young Demetrius? What's it all about, then?"

"Stote's got the Trussetts," explained Jessica.

"Poor beggar," said Lady Blitherwicke. "Is it fatal?"

"No. I mean he's got Rupert Trussett from Turnovers, and his brother Gisborn, to snoop about looking for the shed. And when they find it they'll make a lot of trouble, and Ivor and his mum won't have anywhere to live. Again."

"I see."

"And meanwhile Baked Bean Alley goes ahead as planned."

"Well," I said, slapping my knees and standing up, "the Trussetts aren't the only ones who can snoop about. Jessica and I can do that just as well. Do you happen to know where Stote is at the moment, Lady Blitherwicke?"

"He's out. That's why I was able to sneak away on Jerkin's infernal cycle-machine."

"Excellent. Then we'll see if we can get into his room and have a good look round."

"I see. Yes," said Lady Blitherwicke hesitantly.

"You don't mind, do you?" I asked.

"No, young sausage. Not a bit." She looked down and juggled a twig with her toes. "But if you do find anythin' and it happens to be a book-type thing..."

"Yes?"

"You won't peep, will you?"

Leaving Mum and Lady Blitherwicke to keep an eye on the shed, Jessica and I made our way up to the house. It was much easier to get in this time. Partly because Stote wasn't on the prowl and partly because Lady Blitherwicke had rummaged in the baggy pockets of her cardigan and produced a key.

"This is the key to the front door," she'd told us. "Bally great thing. Like luggin' a spanner around with one. And this is the key to my room. And *this* little chap is the key to the desk drawer. Open it and look under a pile of old Christmas cards. There you'll find the key to the key-cabinet which is on the wall above the desk. The keys for most of the other rooms are in there."

All this had sounded most promising until she'd added that, of course, we wouldn't find a key to Stote's room. He had his own key and always kept those ornate double doors locked. So we didn't bother with any of Lady Blitherwicke's keys (except the one for the front door). We went straight to Stote's room and tried to pick the lock with a bent pin from one of Jessica's badges.

"This is hopeless," said Jessica after a while. "We'll never get in this way."

"Maybe we should try from outside. Through a window."

"There's no time. It'd take us ages to find the right one and we'd be seen and I bet the windows are locked too and..."

"All right," I said. "We won't try a window. So what *shall* we do?"

We didn't get much chance to ponder alternatives. There was the sound of a heavy tread on the staircase round the corner.

"Listen," said Jessica. "Someone's coming."

"Who is it?"

"How should I know. D'you want to go and look?"

"Stote?"

"Very likely," she said. "Right, quick!"

Quick *what*? I thought. We could run down the corridor and round the corner to a part of the house we'd never seen before. Or we could run up the corridor, towards the sound of the footsteps. Which would have been stupid.

Jessica was already tiptoeing off at a smart pace so I followed, heading down the corridor and into the unknown. I skipped round the corner and ran straight into her.

"Don't stop here," I said. "Keep going."

But she didn't keep going. She had one hand over her mouth and was pointing out of a window with the other. Down below us was the broad gravel path which ran along the front of the house. And striding along this path, with a spade over his shoulder, was Stote.

"It's Stote," whispered Jessica, rather pointlessly.

"What's he doing out there?" I asked. "With a spade?"

"Never mind what he's doing out there. Who's just come upstairs?"

"Could be one of the Trussetts," I said.

"Alone? Up here? But why?"

We peered back round the corner. Nothing. No sight or sound. The footsteps could no longer be heard. So we crept back towards Stote's doors and as we edged nearer we began to notice a new sound, this time coming from inside the room. A clicking sound, like small plates being stacked after washing-up.

17

STOTE STICKS HIS NOSE IN

While Jessica and I were making these investigations, things were also starting to happen
back at the shed. Quite pleasant things to
begin with, according to Mum (who told us
all about it afterwards). The fire was
crackling gently; still not enough to boil a
kettle but enough to be friendly. Mum had
overcome her shyness and was showing Lady
Blitherwicke her collection of mugs and
talking her through the pictures in her royal
scrapbook. Lady Blitherwicke kept pointing
out people she knew which was a great thrill
to Mum.

This peaceful scene did not last, however.
One moment they were giggling over a photo
of some old baron who, according to Lady
Blitherwicke, kept white mice in his sock
drawer, and the next they were looking into

the eyes of Stote, who had jumped out of the bushes and was wielding his spade.

"Well, well, well," sneered the butler. "What a jolly party we're having."

"Good grief, Stote," said Lady Blitherwicke. "What are you doin' here?"

"Sticking my nose where it's not welcome," he said and spat into the fire.

"You're dead right there, you bounder. You are indeed most unwelcome."

"Oh dear, oh dear. I'm hurt by that, Lady B. I really am hurt."

"How did you know we were here?"

"Where there's smoke there's fire," said Stote. "And where there's a fire there's a couple of daft old bats sitting round it, drinking tea."

"Well, now you've found us you can go away!"

"But I'm only doing my duty," he said, tightening his grip on the spade. "Someone's built a shed on your land and we can't stand for that, can we? We've got to do something about it."

"You'd better clear off, Mrs D," said Lady Blitherwicke out of the corner of her mouth. "I don't like the look of this."

"Stay where you are," barked Stote.

"No, run for it, Mrs D!"

Mum ran for it but she didn't get very far. She took a few wild steps on the spot as she turned around, looking for an opening, but Stote was in front of her and the shed was behind her. To the right and left, emerging from the greenery at a signal from Stote, were Gisborn and Rupert Trussett.

"Now that," said Stote, "was a silly thing to do. And that," he added, indicating the shed with his spade, "was an even sillier thing to do."

"I gave permission for that shed to be there," said Lady Blitherwicke. "The poor horse has to have somewhere to lay her head and chomp her hay, don't you know."

"Oh really? Why? This shed is completely against every regulation in the book. It's a disgrace. A nightmare. It shouldn't be tolerated. It gets right up Mr Trussett's nose, does this shed. Isn't that so, Mr Trussett?"

"Oh yes," said Gisborn. "There's no two ways about it. I'll have to be down on you for this."

"Like a ton of bricks," said Rupert.

The three men stepped forward, closing the circle round Mum and Lady Blitherwicke. Stote's yellow-grey teeth showed in a grin as he lifted his spade above his head. Then a thought seemed to flutter out of the branches overhead and land in the middle of his brow. (That's what Mum said, anyway.) He hesitated.

"Just one moment," he said, looking round. "Where's that brat of a boy?"

"Shan't tell you," said Mum.

"Rupert, get back to the house and take a look, quick."

Rupert left without a word and Stote smiled at the ladies.

"Shall we get on with the business in hand?" he said.

And he shattered the shed window with one swing of his spade.

18

INTRUDERS

We didn't know about any of this. We were concentrating on the sounds we could hear coming from Stote's room – that peculiar click-clicking – and we were as alert as deer in case they should stop and the doors fly open.

"What is it?" I whispered.

"I've no idea. Take a look."

"Oh no. *You* take a look and I'll watch the corridor." I remembered the last time I'd peeped through that key-hole; when I'd found myself face to face with Stote, and Jessica had been nowhere to be seen. This time she bent down and applied her eye to the door.

"Can you see anything?"

"Yes," she said. "It's ... it's ... I'm not sure what it is."

So I had a look. I wasn't sure at first, either. The room looked much the same as it had before except that now I couldn't see the snooker table. In its place was a large mound of white material, like a full sail, swaying rhythmically from side to side, almost in time with the click-clicking. Sway, pause, click-click.

"What do you make of it?"

"I think," I said, "I think it's someone's bum. Yes. It's someone playing snooker."

"One of the Trussetts?"

"No, no. Too big."

Then the bum moved away from the table. Its owner straightened up and reached out to chalk the cue. I was able to put a face to the bum and a name to the face. Mrs Jerkin.

"Good heavens," I said.

"What?" said Jessica. "Who is it?"

She tried to elbow me aside for another look. I knocked my head against one of the handles and both doors slowly swung open. Mrs Jerkin turned and there was a strange, wide-eyed look on her face. Not anger, but fear.

"I was only having a quick game," she mumbled. "I weren't doing no harm."

We pulled ourselves together and looked quickly about the room. It was a weird feeling, standing there in the middle of all Stote's luxurious belongings. Unnerving. As if at any moment we'd see him sitting in one of the chairs watching us.

"You won't say nothing, will you?" went on Mrs Jerkin. "You won't tell old Stotey? He'll do me good and proper if he finds out."

"How did you get in?" I asked. "The doors were locked."

"I had a little key made, young sir. Old Stotey left his on the kitchen table one day and I pressed it into one of my meat pies..."

"A meat pie?" said Jessica. "But why?"

"So's I could take a copy. My pastry's very good for that kind of thing. A bit on the hard side for eating but all right for copying keys. I didn't steal the key, though, and I didn't mean no harm."

"What did you want it for?"

"Only to have a little go on his snooker table. I love a game of snooker now and again, when Stotey's out."

"Well, you needn't worry about us, Mrs Jerkin," I said. "We have no intention of telling Stote anything."

"Oh, bless you, young sir."

"But you must do us a favour in return," said Jessica. "We need to find something Stote keeps in here."

"Oh no, missy. I can't help you there..."

"It's all right. It doesn't belong to him. It belongs to Lady Blitherwicke and we want to see she gets it back."

"Lady B? How did old Stotey come by it, then?"

"He stole it, Mrs Jerkin. That's how."

"So if you watch the door," said Jessica, "Ivor and I will see if we can see it."

Mrs Jerkin chewed her knuckle for a moment while she thought this over. Then she said, "All right, then. If it's for her Ladyship. Only make it quick. He'll be back soon, I feel it in my bones."

She lumbered over to the door and leaned cautiously into the corridor while Jessica and I searched the room. We pulled out drawers, looked under chairs, behind curtains, in the backs of cupboards. Everywhere we could think of. And found nothing.

"Have you done?" asked Mrs Jerkin anxiously. "Only my bones are giving me a powerful message. Stotey's not far off, I can tell."

"We can't find it," Jessica said. She ran her fingers through her hair and looked hopelessly at me. "What are we going to do now?"

"We'll have to leave it for the moment," I said. "Still, at least we know where we can get a key."

"Yes, but when will we have another chance to use it? And what good will it do anyway? We've looked everywhere already."

"Hurry up, kiddies," moaned Mrs Jerkin from the door. "My bones are giving me proper jip. I can tell there's someone coming."

"Right," I said. "Let's get out of here!"

We dashed for the door but Mrs Jerkin put up a pudgy arm and barred our way.

"Look at this room," she cried, sounding a lot like Mum all of a sudden. "You can't leave it like this."

"But you said there was someone coming!"

"There is, but Stotey'll know you've been in here if you leave it like this."

So we dashed back in and tidied up at a rate I've never tidied up before in my life. A quick glance round told us everything was back in its place. Mrs Jerkin, though, was still barring the way.

"Not yet," she said. "I got to put the snooker table straight!"

"It is straight, woman," said Jessica sharply.

"I know it's straight, missy. But it should be crooked."

"What?"

"It's got a wonky leg. I have to put the wonky leg straight."

"What?"

"I mean, I got to make the straight leg wonky again! Stotey'll know someone's been in if the leg's not wonky."

She shoved past us, applied her shoulder to a corner of the table, removed a book from under the leg and then, red faced and breathless, joined us in the corridor. She gave a deep sigh of relief and turned round to lock the doors.

"Oh blast," she said, suddenly noticing that the book was still tucked under her arm. "I've got to put this blimmin' thing back now."

Jessica and I stared at each other, wide-eyed, as Mrs Jerkin started to open the doors again. I slid the book from under her arm and looked at it. It was a small, worn, leather-bound volume.

On the front, in curly gilt letters, was the single word, *DIARY*.

I blinked at Jessica and opened my mouth to speak, but she was staring over my shoulder with a look of panic on her face. Rupert Trussett was loping silently up the corridor towards us, and he looked as if he didn't intend to ask questions.

19

EXITS AND ENTRANCES

Lady Blitherwicke and Mum watched help-lessly while Stote and Gisborn smashed the shed.

"You worm, you cad, you bally bounder!" Lady Blitherwicke shouted.

"Shut your trap, you daft old bag," said Stote.

Mum told me she was more horrified by these ungentlemanly remarks than she was by the destruction of our new home. She made a little run at Stote and pummelled him on the back.

"Go to it, old horse," cried Lady Blitherwicke in encouragement. "Land him one for me!"

But Stote merely laughed and interrupted his attack on the shed just long enough to push Mum off again. She tottered back and fell down, sobbing with frustration and rage.

Minutes later the shed collapsed on itself

and Gisborn danced on top of the wreckage in triumph.

"This is what happens to sheds that offend the law," he crowed. "This is what happens to the sheds of people who think they can put one over on Turnovers!"

With Rupert galloping after us, we sprinted up the corridor and round the corner once more, Jessica just ahead of me and Mrs Jerkin puffing several paces behind. Then Jessica stopped short and I ran into her. Now what? I thought.

"Why are we running?" she asked.

"Because we've got a Trussett on our tails," I shouted back.

"Yes, but there're three of us and only one Trussett."

"Right," I said, so we turned and rounded the corner again. Just in time to see Rupert collaring Mrs Jerkin.

"Take your hands off me, you oaf," she squealed.

"That's right," said Jessica. "Take your hands off her."

Rupert gave a short laugh. "And what happens if I don't?" he said.

Jessica didn't bother to explain what would happen if he didn't. She punched him on the chin. She had to give a little jump to reach.

"Ow," he said, and blinked.

The blow shocked him more than it hurt him. In fact, I think it hurt Jessica's hand more than Rupert's chin. But it seemed to inspire Mrs Jerkin, who suddenly heaved a meaty elbow into the pit of his stomach. Rupert Trussett gave a sharp wheeze and folded up. We dragged him back down the corridor by his heels, bundled him into Stote's room and locked the door.

"Now what?" said Jessica.

"Back to the shed," I said. "We've got to get the diary to Lady Blitherwicke before we run into Stote."

Of course, back at the shed was exactly where we *would* run into Stote, but we didn't know that. We didn't know the shed was no longer standing, or that Stote and Gisborn Trussett were sitting on what was left of it, gloating over their act of destruction.

But we soon found out.

We were so pleased with ourselves for getting rid of Rupert – and even more for recovering Lord Armitage's diary – that we rushed into the woods without really stopping to think. Mrs Jerkin came with us. She didn't fancy being left alone in the house with Rupert, even though he was locked up.

She did her best to follow but we were eager to give Lady Blitherwicke the good news, so we set a good pace. Mrs Jerkin, who was hardly built for speed, lolloped along for a few metres and then had to stop for breath.

"Be careful, you kiddies," she called after us. "I'm still getting them messages in my bones. It don't feel right. It really don't."

But we were too busy running to bother about her bones. And too excited to take any notice of the strange song that could be heard floating out of the bushes in front of us.

Fifteen men on an old bag's shed!
Yo-ho-ho it's in smithereens!
Bags of dosh to go under the bed!
Yo-ho-ho and a tin of baked beans!

A rotten song, if I ever heard one. Not even really original. I should've been suspicious I know, but my feet were well ahead of my brain. I stumbled into the little clearing where the shed had been. I saw Mum sitting on the ground with her hands over her ears. I saw Lady Blitherwicke with her back turned. Only then did I see where the horrible singing was coming from.

"Ah," said Stote. "It's the Lone Ranger and Tonto. What a lot of pretty badges. Do let me see."

He jumped off the ruined shed and grabbed Jessica's jacket.

"I say, Mr Trussett. Look at this: 'Turnovers Are Tyrants'. What a funny thing to put on a badge."

154

"Turnovers are not tyrants," shouted Gisborn with a stamp of his foot. "And I'll smash anyone who says they are."

Stote laughed like a hyena. I could see that Jessica was thinking of trying the punch to the chin again. I'm glad she thought better of it. Stote still had the spade in his hand and he would've used it, I know he would've.

Then I realized I was still holding Lord Armitage's diary, and I tried to stuff it away under my shirt. My movement was too sudden though and Stote's beady eyes spotted it.

"Where did you get that?" he snapped, letting go of Jessica and striding over to me.

"From Marks and Spencer," I said. "It's cool, isn't it?"

"Not the shirt, smarty-pants. The diary!"

He grabbed a handful of my hair, twisted it and snatched the diary out of my fingers.

"You meddling little thief," he breathed. He wasn't laughing now. His face was creased with anger, and droplets of spittle were running down the wrinkles at the edge of his lips.

"You're the thief," said Jessica. "You stole it in the first place."

"Shut your gob, shorty," said Stote and he gave my hair another painful twist.

We'd been so close to victory and now, in one quick second, Stote had grabbed it back. There were tears of pain in my eyes but they could've been tears of frustration too.

"Now," he said, "what I want to know is what all these silly games are in aid of. Why do you snotty kids keep getting in my way?"

"I'll tell you what they're up to," said Gisborn Trussett. "They want to stop Baked Bean Alley. They're common little vandals."

"But WHY?" bellowed Stote. "Stop Baked Bean Alley? That's stupid, that is. Baked Bean Alley is progress. It's going to be a wonderful palace of a place – a hymn to commerce with a chorus of tinkling cash registers. Baked Bean Alley is going to make my fortune!"

"Money isn't everything, you bally ferret," said Lady Blitherwicke.

"How would you know, rat-bag? You haven't got any!"

And then Mrs Jerkin arrived. Panting and gasping for breath, she blundered on the scene like a frightened elephant. I don't mean to be rude – I *like* old Mrs Jerkin – but that's just what she looked like. And a frightened elephant was exactly what we needed at that point. A look of astonishment crossed Stote's face and he released his grip for a moment. I wriggled and broke free.

"Jerkin, you fat old frump," he yelled. "Get back to the house!"

"Shan't," said Mrs Jerkin. That's about all she could say.

Stote lunged in my direction again. He would've caught me, too, but something stopped him in his tracks. Out of the corner of my eye I saw Mum stoop and grab a shiny, white object at her feet. Then the object came flying through the air and cracked against the top of Stote's skull. He staggered, clutched his head and fell to his knees. The diary fluttered to the ground and Jessica, like a neat little scrum-half, nipped in and whipped it up. Gisborn made a dive for her but Lady Blitherwicke stuck out a noble foot and over he went.

"Quick, Jerkin," she said. "Sit on that man!"

Mrs Jerkin flopped down obediently on top of Gisborn Trussett who made a sound like a squashed bagpipe. She didn't mean to hurt him. I think she was just pleased to take the weight off her feet.

"Now look what you've done," wailed Mum as she picked up the two halves of the mug that had felled Stote. "You've broken my best Princess Di mug. Look at it! Right through the poor dear's nose."

Jessica danced well out of Stote's reach, waving the diary at him in a taunting manner.

"That's done you, Stote," she cried. "You're powerless without this!"

"No!" he snapped back. "I'm not finished yet."

"Oh yes you are. And the Green is saved, isn't it, Lady Blitherwicke?"

"I should bally say so. I'm in charge now!"

"We'll see about that," said Stote. "I can still make my mark. On that twisted old tree, for a start."

"The oak?" I said. "You're not touching that."

"Really? Aren't I? That tree is for the chop, Sonny Jim, diary or no diary!"

And with that he grabbed Mrs Jerkin's bike and started pedalling furiously out of the woods. Leaving us a bit stunned.

I'd thought – I think we all had – that once the diary was back in Lady Blitherwicke's hands, Stote would hang his head like defeated criminals are supposed to. After all, what was the point of giving the go-ahead for Baked Bean Alley if Lady Blitherwicke could just step in and cancel it? Well, if your mind works like Stote's, the point is that you can do one last foul deed before you have to chuck in the towel. As simple as that.

"Oi! That's my bike," said Mrs Jerkin, getting up and releasing Gisborn Trussett.

We were still standing around with bemused looks on our faces as he leapt on Jessica's bike and set off after Stote.

"Wait for me, sir," he called. "I want to see this!"

"After them! Tally-ho!" shouted Lady Blitherwicke.

But Stote and Trussett, with the aid of a good slope, were already weaving through the trees and heading for the drive.

"It's no good, your Ladyship," said Mum. "We'll never catch them now."

"Not on foot, we won't, but we'll soon overtake the blighters in the Bentley. Come on, chaps. 'Once more unto the breach!'"

20

RACE TO
THE GREEN

You could make a good maths problem out of what happened next. If two men are cycling the six kilometres into town at an average speed of twenty kmph, and they are being chased by five people in a Bentley which travels at an average speed of 110 kmph, who gets to town first, the bikes or the Bentley? Remember that the bikes have a one minute start and the five people have to run half a kilometre in the opposite direction at three kmph (which was all Mrs Jerkin could manage) before they can get to the Bentley. You'd probably think it would be a close run thing but the Bentley should still do it. Unfortunately, life isn't like a maths problem. People panic and make mistakes.

For a start, we had a terrible job squeezing everyone into the car. Mrs Jerkin, the last one in, had to sprawl across our laps. Then the car wouldn't start.

"What's the matter with the damn thing?" said Lady Blitherwicke. "Can't hear a sound from the wretched engine!"

"There's no driver," said Jessica, looking round. "We're all in the back seat."

"Oh good grief! Where's the wretched driver got to?"

"Who is the driver?" I asked.

"Blast it," said Lady Blitherwicke. "It's Stote. Right, everybody out. I'll drive."

Both doors flew open and we all tumbled out. Then Lady Blitherwicke dashed into the front seat and started flicking all the controls she could get her fingers on. Mrs Jerkin just managed to tumble back in, last again, as the car coughed and lurched forward.

"You can drive, can you?" asked Jessica nervously.

"Of course I can drive, young bird. A bit."

"A bit?"

"Well, I've watched Stote doin' it. One swishes this wheel thing round and waggles one's feet on these pedals."

"Perhaps we should phone for a taxi," Mum suggested.

But it was too late for that. The Bentley juddered and stopped, juddered and stopped, and then shot down the drive like a rocket. Or almost like a rocket. It wasn't quite as straight.

We skidded towards the main gates, half on the road and half on the verge.

"Breathe in, chaps!" yelled Lady Blitherwicke.

There was a violent scraping of metal as we went through the gates. Then the car swerved to the right and we were all thrown to the left.

"Wrong way!" shouted Jessica.

"I know it's the wrong way but it was the only way I could go without slowin' down."

"Then why not slow down?"

"Because I bally well can't!" yelled Lady Blitherwicke. "Bally back seat drivers!"

So we were whipping along like the wind *away* from town, while Stote and Trussett were getting closer and closer to Turnovers and the destruction of the oak.

"Can't you turn round, Lady Blitherwicke?" I asked. She did turn round. She took her hands off the steering wheel and hooked her elbow over the seat.

"Tell me how to stop, young Demetrius," she said, "then I'll gladly turn round."

"Look out!" yelled Mum and Mrs Jerkin together.

When Lady Blitherwicke turned back to the wheel she saw a van coming towards us.

"What the botheration is he doin' here?" she said, wrenching the wheel.

We lurched across the road, grazed the side of the van and ploughed into a ditch. And stopped. Steam came hissing from under the Bentley's bonnet, as if it were sighing with relief that the journey was over. And the journey was well and truly over. We were wedged into the ditch and the engine was breathing its last.

"Blessed road hog," said Lady Blitherwicke. "How is one supposed to drive with idiots like that comin' at one out of nowhere? What's that smell?"

She turned round and squinted back at the van which had stopped and was throbbing quietly on the empty road.

"Fish," she said. "Of all the humiliation. Shoved off the road by a pesky fish van!"

"It's Dad," cried Jessica.

And, sure enough, there was her father, puffing on his pipe and examining the side of his van. She scrabbled out of the car and ran up to him, shouting and waving.

"Oh, hello," he said slowly, as if he'd perfectly expected to see her there.

"Is it all right?" she asked. "Is the van OK?"

"Well," he said, fingering some black paint marks along the sides, "it's had a bit of a scrape but you can still see the name and that's the main thing, I suppose."

"I mean, does it still go? Does it work?"

"Does it work?"

"Yes. Is the engine all right? Will the wheels turn?"

"Oh yes, I think so."

"Right, everybody," yelled Jessica. "Bundle in. We can still do it!"

Jessica's dad drove the van straight through the Turnovers car park and screeched to a halt on the very edge of the Green. He flung open the doors at the back – we weren't expecting him to be quite so quick – and we tumbled out in a heap. Lady Blitherwicke and Mrs Jerkin flopped about on the grass like beached seals, each in turn managing to pin the other down as she tried to struggle up. I had rolled free but Jessica was somewhere under that mass of woolly arms and legs in baggy stockings.

"Get over there, Ivor," she called. "Quick as you can! They have to be stopped."

I sprinted for the site of Baked Bean Alley and hurdled the orange plastic fencing, ready for action. I wasn't sure what kind of action. Leaping about and shouting and getting in the way, perhaps. I'd think of something. I'd have to. But all was quiet. No sign of Stote. No sign of Trussett. I stood between a pair of yellow diggers, looking round for someone to shout at. The diggers were cold, silent and motionless. Surely, I thought, we can't have got here before Stote? Then a voice called out: "Oi! You aren't allowed in here. Shove off!"

It was ratty old J. Britch, with his clip-board and helmet. He was standing by the oak, with his hand on a chain-saw as big as a motor-bike. My heart went cold at the sight of it.

"Leave that alone!" I shouted. "The project's off!"

"Of course it's not off. We've just been given the emergency go-ahead."

"Don't talk rubbish. There's no such thing."

"Yes, there is. We've just been given it."

"Well, now you're being given the emergency stop. So pack it in."

"Right," he said, flinging his clip-board down and striding away from the chain-saw towards me. "That is it. That is most definitely it. No one speaks to me like that, and I mean *no one*. Understand me, sonny?"

"Yes," I said, taking half a step backwards. "Of course, but..."

"Because anyone who thinks he can talk to me like that," he continued, prodding me in the chest, "can just go and..."

"Stop right there, you clodpole!"

Lady Blitherwicke had reached the plastic fencing and her shrill voice cut through the air like several nails scratching on slate. Jessica was with her but there was no sign of the others. At the sound of Lady Blitherwicke's shriek, Britch hunched his shoulders and winced his eyes shut.

"Look," he said. "Nobody calls me..."

"You bally scallywag," said Lady Blitherwicke, swinging one leg over the plastic fencing as if she couldn't wait to get her hands on him. "I am Lady Marigold Blitherwicke. I own Turnovers and I order you to stop work on this site."

She sounded powerful and decisive – not at all like the Lady Blitherwicke I'd seen on my first visit to the Hall. She would've looked powerful and decisive too if she hadn't got stuck with one foot on either side of the fencing. Jessica helped to bundle her over by tumbling her into a sort of forward roll. She folded in a heap and then sprang up, ready for battle.

Britch watched all this with his mouth hanging open. He turned and blinked at me as if he wanted to say something but couldn't find the words. Then Lady Blitherwicke was striding towards him, pumping her elbows out and leading with her jaw, and that seemed to convince him that she was indeed who she said she was, and meant business. He removed his safety hat and tried to make his ratty face smile.

"I do beg your pardon, your Ladyship," he said, flexing his knees and bending slightly from the waist; half bow, half curtsy. "I was under the impression that one of your representatives..."

"Never mind all that gubbins," said Lady Blitherwicke. "Where's Stote and that other blessed bounder?"

The man opened his mouth to answer but was cut off by a sudden mechanical cough. At first I thought he was choking with embarrassment, but I turned my head slightly and noticed that one of the diggers had started to spit black smoke into the air. It edged towards us and we saw a pale face staring out from the shadows of the cabin.

"Stote," yelled Lady Blitherwicke. "Are you in that blasted machine?"

Silence from Stote. His head was vibrating about in the cabin and you couldn't tell whether he'd pulled his teeth back in a grin or a snarl.

Then there was another cough and the second digger, with Gisborn Trussett at the controls, juddered into life. One behind us and one in front; both advancing with their heavy scoops swinging about like giant heads.

I glanced at Jessica and Lady Blitherwicke, and we side-stepped a little and backed towards the fence. The machines jerked round and followed us.

I began to imagine the worst. Chewed up by mechanical mouths. Squashed into the turf, side by side. Or squeezed through the plastic fencing like sausage meat.

I thought it might please Mum to see my name linked with Lady Blitherwicke's on the "Nine O'clock News", the man with the microphone looking grave while policemen measured up the evidence: "Earlier today, a member of the House of Lords was pressed into service as part of the foundations of the new Turnovers development, Baked Bean Alley. In a bizarre accident, Lady Blitherwicke of Blitherwicke Hall, with two friends from a local school, was flattened by these yellow diggers."

A half turn from the telly man so that the cameras can see the diggers over his shoulder. The policemen look up from their measuring tapes to wave to their families.

"The only witness to the accident," continues the reporter, "was a Mr Stote, a faithful employee of Lady Blitherwicke's."

Faithful? How can they say such things? Stote's pasty face fills the screen, a thin smile beneath his look of false sorrow. "We're all *terribly* shocked, of course. But Lady Blitherwicke has always been right behind the idea of Baked Bean Alley, so it's rather fitting that she's now actually underneath it."

I can't have that, I thought. I can't have Stote sounding off on telly about Lady Blitherwicke *wanting* Baked Bean Alley. Lady Blitherwicke must've been thinking the same thing because she suddenly took a leap at the front of the nearest digger. She'd become a changed woman since she'd got that diary back.

She clambered on to the digger, edging herself along the bonnet until she could press her face against the cabin window. Face to face with Stote. It was the last thing he was expecting. He reversed, slammed on the brakes, twisted this way and that but, once she was on and had taken hold, nothing was going to shake Lady Blitherwicke off. The mechanical arm flailed around helplessly, thrashing here, there and almost everywhere. Except the bit where Lady Blitherwicke was perching. It was as if the digger was trying to touch its nose without bending its elbow. Impossible.

"Stote!" cried Lady Blitherwicke, pressing her face against the window. "You bally bounder! You're goin' to pay for this!"

The other digger hovered for a moment, unsure whether to carry on menacing Jessica and me or to try to help its mate. Stote stuck his head out of his cabin and growled across to it.

"Trussett!"

Gisborn Trussett stuck his head out.

"Yes?"

"Get this dippy old bat off my bonnet!"

"Right, sir."

And Trussett backed his digger away from us, swung its arm at Lady Blitherwicke, missed and thumped into Stote's cabin instead.

"Blunder-bonce!" screamed Stote. "Dolt!"

We could see his thin face wobbling around inside like a TV picture on the blink. Lady Blitherwicke clung on, still shouting names at Stote and hammering on the cabin roof.

169

As Trussett reversed for another go, Stote leapt from his cabin and made for the chain-saw. Jessica and I jumped in his way. He hopped to his left. We skipped to our right. He shimmied to his left again. If it hadn't been for some of the things he was shouting at us, you might've thought we were doing some peculiar country dance. An English summer afternoon, beneath the shade of an old oak tree. Three prancing humans ... and a yellow digger.

And swing your partner round and round
Then crush that chain-saw in the ground...

Which is just what Gisborn Trussett did. There was a grinding and a screeching of torn metal as his digger backed into the dance and straight over the chain-saw.

That's when I *knew* the oak was safe.

I remember turning round to see Jessica's dad strolling across the Green towards us. Behind him were four broad policemen. He was pointing things out to them with the stem of his pipe, quite casually, as if on a country walk.

"That's a bit of meadow-sweet over there," I could imagine him saying, "and you can see a chirpy little wren making a home in that hedge ... and over there we've got a mad butler trying to put together the pieces of a smashed chain-saw..."

21

LADY BLITHERWICKE BOUNCES BACK

The next time Jessica and I saw Lady Blitherwicke, was back in her own room a week later. The furniture was under dust-sheets and Lady B herself was up a ladder. She was busy scraping flakes of old paint from the wall.

"Hello, you scallywags," she called down to us, wiping her face with her apron. "How're tricks with you?"

"We're fine," said Jessica. "We just thought we'd see how you were getting on."

"Oh, toppin', young bird. Absolutely toppin'. I've discovered a new thing, you know. Do-It-Oneself, it's called. Decoratin' and stuff. Just what the old place needs now that you-know-who is clapped in irons in some dusty cell."

"About that diary," said Jessica. "Was it really full of wicked secrets?"

Straight out with it. Just like that. I mean, I know I'd been wondering but I would never have come straight out with it.

"That's the funny thing, Jessica," said Lady Blitherwicke, clambering down the ladder. "No, it wasn't. It was full of cricket scores and averages and notes about makin' cheese. Very keen on cheese-makin', was Lord Armitage. Lot of fuss and worry over nothin' if only we'd known. Still, that's all water under the bridge now."

She wandered over to the corner and blew into the speaking-tube.

"Mrs Jerkin?" she shouted into it. "Pot of tea for three, if you wouldn't mind. And a nosebag of Bobbly-Oddbods. Many thanks."

"We don't want to interrupt if you're busy," I said.

"Nonsense, young gum-boot. Always welcome. Always welcome. You must know that."

She swished a dust-sheet aside so that we could sit down. There was a briskness in her movements, a sparkle about her that I would never have thought possible a fortnight ago. I had the feeling that we'd done more than save the Green: we'd helped to save Lady Blitherwicke, too. Quite by accident.

"One has plans for this place, you know," she said with a wink. "Blitherwicke Hall is the kind of hole where people can have adventures. Don't you think?"

172

She pulled a couple of sketch-maps from under the sofa and unrolled them on the floor, talking the whole time. She hardly stopped.

"All this is too big for one old biddy," she said, tapping the map. "Out here, in the woods. See? Bags of room for beasts of all kinds. And walks for the humans. Here, here and here. Then, indoors –" flinging that map aside and turning to the other one – "People like a bit of a chase now and then. Plenty of space out there in the corridors for romps and adventures. Up and down all those bally stairs."

"For the public, you mean?" asked Jessica.

"For the public, of course, young bird. Make use of the place. Same as the other place. Tip-unders, Overturns..."

"Turnovers?" I suggested.

"That's the chap. Got plans for that, too," she said, rummaging under the sofa for another rolled-up map. "At one end, a shop with shopkeepers who speak to the customers. I mean *speak* to them. No security and definitely no music. At the other end, a kind of race track. For trolleys. So one can biff around the place without havin' to stop and buy things. A few obstacles, perhaps: bales of straw, water traps. That kind of thing, don't you know?"

"And no Baked Bean Alley," said Jessica.

"I should bally well say not. *Absolutely* no Baked Bean Alley. Which means the Green is safe. Cricket and kites and wot-not."

"And tree-climbing," I added.

She chortled and gave us each a punch on the arm.

"I'd like to say how grateful I am..." I went on.

"Poppycock, young Demetrius."

"Yes, but I *am* grateful and I would like you to know that. In fact, I've made up a song about it."

"I say!" said Lady Blitherwicke.

I thought I heard Jessica groan but I decided to ignore her. I'd spent ages putting this song together, sitting on a branch in the oak, absorbing the natural rhythms of the breeze and the birds. It was an attempt to sum up all I felt about the saving of the Green.

"What's it called, young song-thrush?"

"It's called 'The Ballad of Baked Bean Alley'," I said.

Lady Blitherwicke closed her eyes, I cleared my throat and began.

Well, they ain't gonna forget
The Battle of Baked Bean Alley.
No, they ain't gonna forget...

"I don't think so, Ivor," said Jessica.

"What?"

"Not singing, thank you. I don't think it helps."

"Oh. Had he started, then?" asked Lady

Blitherwicke, opening her eyes and looking round.

"But this is for posterity," I told them. "People shouldn't forget what nearly happened to the Green. And, anyway, there's twelve verses to go..."

"That's the trouble, though," said Jessica. "People will *try* to forget if you make noises like that."

"It's not a noise, Jessica. It's my way of saying thank you to Lady Blitherwicke..."

"Don't mention it, old cod-fish. No need. No need at all. Point taken and all that. Let's not make a song and dance over it."

And just then Mrs Jerkin came in with the tea. So that was that. If people have to choose between a cup of tea and a bit of culture, they'll always go for the tea. Even the Upper Classes.

You know, I don't think I ever managed to get right through a single one of my songs during the Battle of Baked Bean Alley. Someone always interrupted. People don't understand. They didn't understand Mozart and now they don't understand me. I can't help wondering whether things might not have been a lot easier if I'd been able to sing my "Lost Green Blues" straight through in the first place. It might just have done the trick.

Still, I suppose there's nothing to stop me now, is there? I mean, the story's told and it might finish things very nicely if I just ran through all twelve verses of "The Ballad of Baked Bean Alley". Don't you agree? Right. Don't go away.

Well, they ain't gonna forget
The Battle of Baked Bean Alley.
No, they ain't gonna forget...